# Yellow Ribbon

## Second Edition

# Yellow Ribbon

## Second Edition

## Mike Faricy

Library of Congress Control Number: 2023914633
paperback ISBN: 978-1-962080-11-8
e-book ISBN: 978-1-962080-13-2


MJF Publishing books may be purchased for education, Business, or promotional use. For information on bulk purchases, please contact the author directly at mikefaricyauthor@gmail.com


Published by

MJF Publishing
https://www.mikefaricybooks.com

*To Teresa*

**"That's about as useful as a chocolate teapot!"**

# Acknowledgments

I would like to thank the following people for their help and support:
Special thanks to my editors, Kitty, Donna and Rhonda for their hard work, cheerful patience and positive feedback.

I would like to thank Ann and Julie for their creative talent and not slitting their wrists or jumping off the high bridge when dealing with my Neanderthal computer capabilities.

Special thanks to Ann for her patience.

Last, I would like to thank family and friends for their encouragement and unqualified support. Special thanks to Maggie, Jed, Schatz, Pat, Av, Emily and Pat for not rolling their eyes, at least when I was there, and most of all, to my wife Teresa whose belief, support and inspiration has from day one, never waned.

# One

I'd been up with Heidi until almost sunrise. Not a complaint, by the way, more like bragging. Every so often, she gets this insatiable hormonal swing that might last about twenty-four hours. It was incredible—if you could survive. Then, while recovering on my couch at home, I got the call to come over and join the girls. A call? Let's be honest, it was a plea, begging, how could I refuse? It was just that after the previous night of virtually no sleep, I was really running on empty.

I arrived at their town-home late in the afternoon. The rooms had all been painted in the past year. I knew because I'd done the work, then been paid by way of some great dinners. The place was spotless, nice furniture, not necessarily expensive, but nice all the same and certainly not threadbare.

The girls and I settled into the living room. The drapes were pulled, it was very private. At first, we just talked and watched a little TV. Then we ate a simple dinner in the living room, occasionally glancing at the TV, but really just involved in casual conversation and catching up. One thing seemed to lead to another, and now, once I finished the last of my beer, it would be time for me to join them. From where I was sitting, I could hear the laughter.

They'd been in the bathroom for the past twenty minutes chatting away while waiting for me. There were two of them. Sisters. Beautiful. A blonde and a redhead, Emma and Ava. I kept getting them mixed up, I always did, screwing up who was who. Not that they seemed to be bothered. On the contrary, they seemed to think it was kind of funny. They'd both claim to be the other, which didn't help in solving any of my confusion.

"You called me that the last time, I already told you, I'm Emma," the redhead said with a straight face.

"Dev?" the blonde would ask. "How come you always call us by the wrong name?"

Occasionally one of them called out to me from the bathroom and told me to hurry up or asked me when I was going to come in and join them. I remained on the couch, still trying to recharge my batteries from my Heidi marathon.

I finally figured I'd left them alone long enough. I rolled my shoulders a couple of times, then turned my head from side to side, cracking my neck, getting ready to face the music, and not really sure how I was going to handle both of them. I set my empty beer bottle on the living room carpet next to the couch where we'd been playing around earlier. I took a deep breath, steadied myself, and began to head down the hallway approaching the bathroom door with a fair degree of caution.

The door was half open, and as I drew closer, I could hear the two of them in there whispering, giggling, and making plans while sitting in the Jacuzzi. Light from the half dozen scented candles they'd insisted on lighting flickered out the bathroom doorway and into the hall.

"What's taking him so long?"

"I don't know. He's always late."

"He better get here pretty soon."

"Let's splash him when he comes."

"We can hide under the bubbles, and he won't see us."

"Yeah, and then we'll splash him."

That seemed to get them going all over again and they started laughing and splashing one another as I tiptoed toward the door.

"Are you two ready for me?" I called from the hallway.

That brought on squeals of delight, and they both screamed, "Hurry up, Dev. Hurry up."

As I slowly opened the door, I gave a little evil laugh which brought on a series of shrieks, and they slid down in the Jacuzzi beneath about a foot of bubbles until just their heads were exposed.

"You promised you'd get in with us," Emma screamed, or was it Ava? I had them mixed up again, anyway it was the blonde.

"Yeah, Dev, come on, you said you would," the redhead pleaded, then splashed some water and blew a handful of bubbles toward me.

"All I know is, I promised your mom you'd have a bath and be in bed before she got home from her class," I said.

They scooted over to the far side of the Jacuzzi shrieking, and then the two of them started kicking and splashing.

"Come on, now who's gonna be first?" I said and grabbed a thick white towel from the rack on the opposite wall. The floor was already under about a half-inch of water from all their splashing.

"Me, me."

"No, that's not fair let me, it's my turn, you always get to be first, Emma. It's my turn."

"I get to go first because I'm the oldest, and that makes me the boss."

That seemed to click something in my brain, and I repeated, *Emma, oldest, blonde,* to myself a half-dozen times. Then I spread my arms, holding the thick bath towel and shaking it from side to side.

"Okay, now we've got two towels. How about both of you getting out at the same time, and then everyone can be first? How does that sound?"

That brought on more shrieks and giggles as they hurried to climb out over the slippery edge of the Jacuzzi, in the process spilling a couple gallons of water across the white hexagonal tiles of the bathroom floor. A wave of water and bath bubbles washed over my shoes.

"Careful now, we don't want anyone slipping and falling. Take your time, this floor is wet and slippery."

Of course, they completely ignored my wise advice. I threw the towel over blonde, five-year-old Emma's head. Then I reached back and grabbed the towel for Ava. In the process, I lowered my knee, and the leg of my jeans dipped into the water pooled on the bathroom floor. I wrapped the towel around little four-year-old Ava as she stood there shivering.

"Come on now. We'll dry off in your bedroom where it's nice and warm, and then you can both get into jammies."

"I get to pick the story. I know which one to get," Emma shouted and then dashed out of the bathroom.

"No me, it's my turn tonight. Don't pick the one I want, Emma. You can't," little Ava shouted as she started to take off in hot pursuit. She slipped on the floor. Fortunately, I somehow managed to catch her as she fell. She missed the edge of the Jacuzzi with her forehead by just a fraction of an inch. She giggled as I caught her, like her near death-accident was all just a big game. I hoisted her up on my shoulder, and we followed Emma into their bedroom.

"You can't pick my book, Emma," Ava reminded as we stepped into the bedroom.

"I'm going to pick an even better one," Emma said.

"What one? What one are you picking?"

"You can both pick a book, but before we pick books, we need to have pajamas on first."

Who knew slipping a little flannel nightie on could take the better part of ten minutes? Probably most moms, but I sure didn't have a clue. Once the nighties were on, we had to go into the kitchen so they could each have a sip of water. I said no to another cookie, but then decided all three of us could probably do with one, I snuck a second when the girls weren't looking. They picked out their books, said their prayer's including one for me, gave kisses all around, and finally snuggled under the covers.

"Read mine first, read mine," Emma said just as the doorbell rang.

"No me, read mine first," Ava said and then made a face at her sister.

The doorbell rang a second time, and I muttered to myself wondering who it could be as I left the bedroom to answer the door.

A fat guy with dark, curly hair was standing at the door, his back was to me, and he looked like he was scanning the street. My first thought was he must be a neighbor because he was just wearing shirt sleeves, and it was fairly cool for an early October evening. As I opened the door, he turned toward me, a look of shocked surprise washed across his face the moment he saw me.

"Oh, sorry, I was looking for Isabella, does she still live here?" he asked then leaned to the side to look past me and check out the living room.

"Yeah, she does," I said. My initial impression was I didn't like this guy.

"Well then, who the hell are you?"

"Carlos, mommy said you weren't supposed to come back to our house, ever again. You were bad, Carlos, very bad, and you're not supposed to be here," Emma said from somewhere behind me.

I turned to look at a very angry, red-faced Emma just as little Ava peeked out from behind her older sister with a wide-eyed stare. A second later, I saw stars when he blindsided me.

Based on the way my face looked once I came to, he landed a few more punches before he was finished.

The front door was open, the girls were gone, I could only see out of one eye, my lips were swollen, I tasted blood, had one hell of a headache, and Isabella was just pulling up in front.

# TWO

The paramedic said, "I'd say you have a slight to moderate concussion," I was sitting on the couch, holding a gelled ice pack to the side of my throbbing head. He was kneeling on the floor next to me and in the process of taking a blood pressure cuff off my arm.

As he spoke, he carefully folded the blood pressure cuff and placed it back into a blue case with a red cross on the front.

"At least your nose doesn't seem to be broken, that swelling around the eye should go down in the next thirty-six hours. Maybe keep it iced off and on for the next day or two, and that will help. I'd stay away from spicy foods for the next couple of days with those lips," he laughed. "How's the breathing, any troubles with that nose?"

"You mean can I? Through my nose? Yeah, it'll be okay, I guess. Just trying to clear my head is all, still kind of dizzy, things are spinning a little."

There had to be a half dozen cops in the small town-house. I could see Isabella at her dining room table occasionally glancing over at me. She was red-eyed, crying, and nodding to some guy in a suit and tie seated across the table from her. He was typing on a notebook of some sort. What looked like a cellphone sat on the table between the two of them, I guessed it was probably recording their conversation. Isabella was nodding, then biting her lower lip. She did not look happy.

It was dark outside, but at least two more police officers were out front, apparently walking back and forth across the front yard with flashlights. A couple of red and blue lights were flashing on top of squad cars out in the street. The lights were shining through the windows, bouncing off the living room walls, and in general, adding to my pounding headache.

"I don't think we'll need to transport you. Well, unless you want us to. But, if I were you, I'd think about going down to the ER and getting checked out. Maybe have somebody drive you down there, preferably tonight. If you don't go down tonight, I'd certainly get in there tomorrow, just to play it safe."

"Thanks," I said, nodding slowly while my head continued to throb, having no intention of going to the ER either tonight or tomorrow.

"I really think you should, sir," he said, reading my mind.

"Appreciate the advice. Mind if I go over and join them at the table. I'm sure they'd like to ask me the same questions a few more times."

"Yeah, sure, we're done here, just take it easy the next couple of days, you got pretty banged up. It looks pretty shitty, but you're awfully lucky, it doesn't seem to be as bad as it looks."

"Thanks for checking me out," I said, then groaned to my feet and took some unsteady steps toward the crowd gathered around the dining room table. I slowly approached, then ran my hand across Isabella's shoulder as I sat down in the chair next to her. She gave my hand a quick squeeze, glanced over at me, and tears immediately started running down her cheeks.

With the mascara and eyeshadow pooled around her eyes, she looked like she'd gone twelve rounds with someone a lot larger than her demure little frame. Her always perfect dark hair seemed limp and bedraggled. There was a pile of Kleenex on the table in front of her, and she held more in her hand.

"Oh, Dev," she said and sniffled when she looked at me then put her hand up to gently touch the side of my face.

I reflexively jerked my head back, which got things really spinning, and I had to grab onto the edge of the table and close my good eye for a long moment until things settled down.

"I'm so sorry," she said and started crying again.

A couple of the uniform cops and the suit at the table looked over at me. My wobbly entrance into the dining room was not exactly the sort of thing that would instill confidence.

"I know you're not at your best, Mr. Haskell. Maybe just rest for a minute or two and think if there's anything else you can add to your previous statement?" the suit said. He looked to be about forty and gave the immediate impression he was not someone to be trifled with. He had dark hair, shaved along the sides up to where a part would normally be, the hair was immediately longer and combed over on the top of his head. He had big, solid-looking hands like he had done labor or maybe farm work early on. He had introduced himself to me earlier, but with all the spinning and the fireworks going off in my head, I couldn't remember his name.

I began to shake my head indicating I didn't want to wait and my skull immediately felt like it was going to explode. I waited a few seconds for the fireworks to stop inside then said, "I don't think I can add anything else, it all happened so fast. It couldn't have been a minute, maybe more like just a few seconds. I don't know what he hit me with, his fists, a bottle, I just don't know. Like I said, I thought he was a neighbor, you know, because he was just in shirt sleeves."

"Mister O'Kelly?"

"Who?"

"Mister O'Kelly, Carlos O'Kelly was the man who assaulted you," The suit looked over at Isabella as she nodded.

"Oh, yeah, sorry, as matter of fact, Emma called him that, Carlos. Said he was bad and wasn't supposed to be here. I turned around to look at her for half a second, and then the lights went out. I didn't know his last name. Like I said, I figured he must have just run over from next door."

"And you were babysitting the little girls?"

"That's right."

"Have you done that before?"

"Yeah, but just once or twice in a pinch," I said, glancing over at Isabella. That started things spinning again, and I took a couple of deep breaths before proceeding. "I've known Isabella since we were in high school. Her husband, Danny, and I were pals. I guess the sitter canceled for tonight." I was going to look over at Isabella but decided to just hold my head still.

"Like I said before," Isabella jumped in. "She called about a half-hour before I was supposed to leave and said she had the flu. That's really the last thing we needed here, flu. So, it was such short notice I couldn't think of who to call, so I called Dev. The girls know him, and he ran right over, it was just going to be for a few hours, not late, it's only a two-hour class. We usually meet for about thirty minutes before class for a coffee and a quick review."

"Where's your husband?"

"Operation Enduring Freedom," she scoffed.

"He's in the service, deployed?"

"No, he's dead," Isabella said.

"Afghanistan, Helmand province, 2011," I added.

"I'm sorry," the suit said.

Isabella nodded and dabbed her eyes again with the Kleenex.

There was a noticeable silence for a couple of beats before one of the uniforms behind me asked, "Do you have a jacket here, Mr. Haskell?"

"My jacket? Yeah, it's a brown leather bomber's jacket. It's hanging up in the front closet."

One of the cops stepped over and pulled the bifold door open on the closet in the entryway. The door was louvered and painted white. It gave a high-pitched squeak as he pulled it open, and the sharp pain in my head seemed to immediately ratchet up with the sound.

"A brown bomber jacket? Doesn't seem to be anything like that hanging in here now."

"It should be on a hanger in there, got a Ranger tab on the left shoulder, it's next to a little pink ski jacket if I remember correctly."

"I see the ski jacket, but there's no brown leather jacket in here."

I thought for half a second, swallowed to keep my stomach down, and said, "My car keys were in there. Can you check and see if my car is out front? It's a black Infiniti QX, two-thousand-five. It's got silver wheel rims, and the taillight on the passenger side is taped over with red tape. There's a crack down the passenger side of the windshield, oh, and a big crease along the passenger side."

The cop stuck his head out the front door then called back in the room, "Did you park it nearby?"

"Are you shitting me? It should be right out front at the curb. I parked it in front of the house," I said, groaning as I slowly got back up on my feet. I had to steady myself on the dining room chair for half a moment.

I worked to keep the contents of my stomach down as I walked to the front door and looked out. There was a police squad with flashing red and blue lights parked exactly where I had left my car. The lights immediately set off a wave of nausea, and I had to close my eyes again until things settled down.

"God damn it, I don't suppose you guys had it towed, did you?" I asked the suit standing right behind me. My question sounded more like I was pleading, hoping they'd moved my car for some reason.

"No, we didn't. You know your license number?"

"Yeah, Minnesota, F-N-L," I said then gave him what I thought was the number. "I'm sorry, I'm still a little foggy, pretty sure the letters are right, but the numbers, I'm not so sure, it's either seven-four-nine or seven-nine-four. I just can't seem to focus too clearly at the moment."

"That's okay, will have it in just a second, you're calling it in, Joey?" he said to the uniform standing next to him and already on the radio attached to his shoulder.

The guy nodded then looked at me. "Haskell, H-A-S-K-E-L-L, first name Devlin. Yeah, two-thousand-five Infiniti QX, black. Did you say there was a rear taillight broken?"

"Yeah, on the passenger side, a crack from top to bottom on the passenger side of the windshield, and then that crease across the passenger side doors."

He nodded, then turned and said something else into his radio, but I couldn't pick up what it was.

"Maybe come back and sit down at the table, Mr. Haskell. I'm sure you're hurting, but we need to get as much information as quickly as we can."

"Not a problem."

"You're a pal of Lieutenant LaZelle's aren't you?"

I was about to nod, but my head was throbbing so hard I didn't dare. "Yeah, we go way back to when we were kids. I was always the better hockey player," I said then gave a throaty groan as I sat down.

"I'll be sure to remind him."

I proceeded to answer questions for the better part of the next hour, but I don't think I was much help.

# Three

It was well after midnight. There was an attractive uniformed female officer named Patty Ryan, who had been assigned to spend the night at Isabella's. She arrived maybe an hour earlier and more or less taken charge. She'd picked up glasses and cups from the coffee table, the dining room, all over the kitchen and loaded the dishwasher. She straightened up the kitchen, got the usually spotless living room back into a semblance of order, all the while attending to Isabella and helping her maintain at least a degree of sanity.

Just now, she was making a fresh pot of coffee. Officer Patty and I, along with the other officers, were working to keep Isabella away from the coffee. The paramedics had left some sleep aids, and Isabella had taken one maybe a half-hour ago. She'd been fighting sleep ever since. That sleep aid could kick in anytime now, and it would be just fine with me.

"God, if I'd known he was out there, I never would have left the girls," Isabella said, not for the first time. She had pretty much cried herself out over the past few hours, but that didn't stop her from repeating the same mantra over and over again, blaming herself for something that was clearly out of her control.

"When you told me a while back that your ex-boyfriend was in Pleasant Lake, I thought you meant a house, you know actually on the lake. It never dawned on me he was in rehab."

"Hardly a boyfriend, more like a bad encounter that kept coming back to haunt the three of us. It was one of the conditions of his going back into rehab again instead of the workhouse. They were supposed to inform me of his release at least a week in advance of the date."

"Well, I guess with your new phone number, it looks like that might have fell through the cracks."

"The information we have is that he wasn't released. He just walked away, again, without completing the twenty weeks. Apparently, he's done that before," the detective at the table said.

"Walked out of a rehab facility?" I asked.

"Yeah," Isabella said. "He's done it at least twice that I know of and now this, God. I suppose that means there's a fourth trip to rehab somewhere in his future, plus he'll have to do the workhouse time for the bounced checks."

"I think, under the circumstances, the state might just have a little different plan for his future. I'm sure the girls are all right, he'll come to his senses and bring them home anytime now," I said

"You really think so?" She sounded like she was grasping at the only straw out there in a very large cesspool of sludge.

"Yeah, we'll have a big welcome home party for them, with two cakes, and we'll invite all their friends," I said, waiting for her to smile. Instead, her lower lip began to tremble, and suddenly, there was another flood of tears. Under the circumstances, who could blame her?

The pounding in my head had gone from being constant to more of a lightning strike mode. Things seemed to be settling down for a moment or two, and then, suddenly this searing pain would race back up my neck and blast across my skull exploding on the right side of my brain like an artillery shell. I made my way over to the refrigerator and exchanged the room temperature gel-pack I'd been holding for the cold one I pulled off the freezer shelf.

When I closed the freezer door Officer Patty shot me a look, then walked over and quietly said, "You both should try and get some rest. You're going to have a busy day tomorrow."

"Do you think he'll call?" Isabella asked again.

Officer Patty shook her head and said, "I don't know. I do know that whether or not he calls, we're going to need you, and the girls are especially going to need you, both of you, to be at your very best. Now, you need to get some rest. Don't worry. We're here if your phone rings or someone's at the door, so why don't you just try and close your eyes for a bit."

"I don't think I can," Isabella said.

"You need to try, Is," I said. "I'll flake out on the couch. If anything happens one of us will get you. But, she's right, you've got to be sharp tomorrow, we both do. The girls need you to be at your very best, and you won't be able to do that if you don't get some sleep. So come on, try and close your eyes. We both should."

"I won't be able to sleep."

"Then just rest, but you have to give it a try. You'll be no good tomorrow if you don't try. Come on," I said and then put my arm around her shoulder and guided her down the hallway to her bedroom.

"Are you going to be here in the morning?"

"Yeah, I will be, and then once you're settled, I'm going to help look for the girls. But before any of that happens, you need to get some rest."

"Okay, okay, I'll try. I'm really sorry he did that to you, Dev," she said and indicated my swollen face with a nod of her head.

"Don't worry about it, looks worse than it really is, you've got more than enough on your plate right now."

"Do you think they'll be alright, the girls?"

"They'll be okay. I'm sure Emma is giving him directions right now."

"Oh, God, one time, he yelled and called her a bossy little bitch," she said, and a tear ran down her cheek.

"Don't you worry about that, Is. They'll be fine and probably home sooner than you think. And then we're going to throw the two of them the biggest party you've ever seen."

"I just don't know."

"Well, I do, and like Officer Patty said, you need to get some rest. I'll just be out there on the couch. I'll come get you if anything happens. I promise, so you just lie down and close your eyes. You don't have to sleep, but you do have to try and get some rest, okay?"

"Sorry about your face, you really look like shit."

"You just get some rest," I said.

I closed the door to her room and went back out to the living room. I stretched out on the couch and pulled a leopard skin fleece blanket up over me. I turned onto my left side then cautiously laid the gel pack on the right side of my face and hoped for the best. I closed my eyes, and things started to spin for a moment or two, then settled back down. I drifted off to sleep, hoping a little rest might alleviate some of the pounding and fireworks in my head.

According to the digital clock on the stove, it was just a little after five when I got up and walked into the kitchen. Officer Patty was on an iPad and looked like she was in the process of sending an email. I half leaned over to see if I could get her email address, but the screen had changed.

"Any news?" I half-whispered, afraid even the slightest noise might wake Isabella.

She shook her head. "No, at least not so far. Don't worry. We'll get those girls back safe and sound."

"What an absolute asshole," I half said to myself.

"Yeah, that pretty much sums it up. Based on the list of priors I've seen, he looks like the poster child for spoiled little rich kid. I've seen this kind of history before. It's hard to believe, but he's probably a bigger disappointment to himself than to anyone else. So how's the head?"

"Actually, better, at least the constant pounding seems to have stopped for the moment. Now it seems to be in direct relation to just moving my head too fast. This is just about the worst I've ever had."

"He really nailed you. You're lucky there wasn't more damage, you don't mind me saying, it looks like shit."

"I can't wait to discuss that fact with him."

"No doubt, but if you really intend to help, just let us deal with this butthead, he's not about to see the light of day once we get hold of him. And we will get him. Then, you can visit him and tell him what an idiot he is, but for right now, the best way you can help is by not helping. You should maybe try and get some more rest, it can only improve your condition, and we're going to need you sharp as well as Isabella."

"Hear anything from her room?"

Officer Patty shook her head. "They take about forty minutes or so to kick in, but once those pills from the paramedics start working, she could be out for a few more hours. You wouldn't want to make them a steady diet, but for tonight, under these circumstances, it's just what she needed."

# Four

Just as Officer Patty opened the front door and cautioned whoever was out there to be quiet, I came awake on the living room couch. I kept my eyes closed for a moment and listened. I recognized Aaron LaZelle's familiar voice as he stepped into the living room, talking softly and trying not to wake me. We'd known one another since we were kids playing hockey, and I knew the suit who'd been directing the questioning last night reported directly to him. I opened my eyes just as another uniform stepped into the living room right behind Aaron. The uniform was a big guy, and his jacket covered up the name stitched on his uniform shirt.

"No need to pretend you're nice by talking softly," I said and slowly sat up.

"Man, you look like shit," Aaron said.

I smiled.

"Didn't we teach you to duck? So how's the head? How you feeling?"

"I'll make it. You got any news for us?"

He shook his head slightly. "Nothing yet, we got everyone in town looking for your vehicle. We're doing rousts on all known contacts of this Carlos O'Kelly, character. Something will click sooner or later, and things will take off. We just need a little break is all."

I'd heard him give a version of that speech more than a few times in the past. Based on my experience, in reality, what he was saying was, "We are royally screwed for the time being."

"Known associates? You mean barflies, idiots?"

"Yeah, along with family and anyone else we can think of. We're checking everyone and everything, believe me, Dev. I've had teams out rousting folks all night long, and they're not about to stop. Something's bound to turn up, and we'll have those two little girls back just as soon as possible."

"What about the feds?"

"At this stage, I'd prefer not to go there, but we're keeping an eye on that option. The moment it looks like we're losing control, they'll get the call to come in. I don't have any problem with that."

"Do you even have control now? Have you, have we, even for a moment, been in control?"

"Believe me, I understand what you're saying, and I share your frustration, we all do. But this isn't your standard snatch and grab. We haven't heard anything from this idiot, no contact, nothing like a ransom demand, no taunting phone calls, zip. We're still looking at this as a really bad domestic."

"No calls, no contact, what does that tell you?"

"It strongly suggests an impulse reaction. I think if he looks back with some honest, soul searching reflection, he'll start to see the mistakes he's made and find a way to get the girls back to their mother. Then, he'll probably try and hightail it out of town. At which point, we'll grab his ass and lock him up in a dark hole for the rest of his remaining days."

"Honest, soul searching reflection? You got a hell of a lot more faith than I do."

"Faith? No, nothing to do with faith, Dev. Just good hard work that will let us catch a break. That's all we need, one break, Dev. Just one, and then we got this jackass by the short hairs."

I stupidly shook my head, and the pounding suddenly started up again then launched into the fireworks exploding on the right side of my brain.

"You okay?"

"Yeah, just a momentary short in the system," I said.

"There's liable to be another problem, as well," Aaron said after waiting a long moment.

"What's that?"

"Word seems to have gotten out, so the news media is going to be camping on the doorstep here."

"That won't help, Isabella doesn't need all that going on right now. Can't you lock them up or something?"

"We can post someone out front, a squad, at least keep them more or less at bay, if not away. For starters, don't talk to them. Don't give a comment. Don't even let them wish you good luck. Just keep it buttoned up."

"Maybe it would be a good idea if we got Isabella out of here before they show up? You know, so she could avoid them completely."

"No," Aaron said. "First of all, if Carlos plans to phone or somehow make contact, this is the place to be. Secondly, she needs to be here, in surroundings that are familiar to her. And, well, there's still the hope that he might just bring the girls back here. We won't leave her alone. Someone is going to be here with her for the foreseeable future. I'm guessing under the circumstances she's probably had just a couple hours of sleep, fitful at best. How are you doing, by the way?"

"Me? I look a lot worse than I feel at this stage. Sacking out for a bit seemed to help. I get another twenty-four hours under my belt, and I should be back to normal."

"Whatever that is."

I ignored that last comment. "Now, what can I be doing to help?"

Aaron looked at me and shook his head. "Here's what would really help. Please, do absolutely nothing. Please. In fact, the less you do, the better. Well, unless you remember something that slipped your mind last night when Ditter interviewed you. Then we'll want to hear from you, otherwise stay the hell away."

"Ditter, that was the guy's name? I mean, he told me, probably more than once, but I was having trouble focusing, to tell you the truth."

"Yeah, Jack Ditter, he's good, Dev, very good. He's my best, which means you don't have to help. We'll call you if we need you. Okay? So, Have you been checked out?" " Aaron said, changing the subject.

"Me? Yeah, the paramedics were here, they gave me something for the headache. Twenty-four hours will probably be the best thing for me, that and getting those little girls back home safe and sound. Once this swelling goes down, I'll be back to my perfect self."

"You should see a doctor, Dev. Probably a psychiatrist, too, but certainly a doctor just to get checked out and be sure."

"Once those girls are back, I will, I promise."

"I mean this as a friend, Dev we don't want you involved. This is delicate. We're working it the best we can. No one can do a better job, Dev, we've got the resources. So please, do not get involved. You'll only be screwing things up. I hope I'm making myself clear?"

"Yeah, not to worry. I understand, relax, and take a chill pill, man. I plan to stay cool, very cool."

"Please, see that you do."

"I said I would, I promise."

"I'm holding you to that, Dev."

Aaron was still there when Isabella came out of her bedroom. She looked and sounded groggy almost like she'd been drugged, which, upon reflection, I guess was pretty much the case. Officer Patty said her good-byes, told us to hang in there and that she'd be back for the late shift if it was needed. She was relieved by another great looking female uniform, Officer Vang.

"Let's keep it simple. Just call me Tai," she said. Then she proceeded to make a fresh pot of coffee and opened up a box filled with fresh croissants. She placed the box on the dining room table. "My aunt and uncle own a bakery over on University Ave. We all had to work there as kids."

"I thought you cops just ate doughnuts."

She shot a smile at me that was meant to be anything but charming.

Aaron reached in and grabbed a croissant, then took a sip of hot coffee. It dawned on me that he'd been working through the night and was as exhausted as Isabella looked and at least as tired as I felt, he'd had absolutely no sleep and probably no break in the action for the immediate future.

The uniform who had arrived with Aaron removed his jacket, nodded at Isabella and said, "I'm Gary Johnson, I've got a list of people we've been talking to. I'd like you to take a look and see if there might be anyone we've missed, maybe a name that might pop up we hadn't considered or maybe someone we should reconsider."

Aaron sat down at the dining room table and rubbed his face as Johnson handed a two-page list across the table. He looked as tired as Aaron, and I guessed he'd probably been rousting folks out of bed for the past ten hours, not exactly the best way to win a popularity contest.

Isabella quickly ran down the list, then turned to the second page and said, "To tell you the truth, I only recognize a couple of these names. I think this Luci O'Kelly is his grandmother, isn't she?"

"His grandmother?" Johnson said and shot a look at Aaron. "Mrs. O'Kelly is in an assisted living facility, suffering from Alzheimer's. She was unable to be much help. She's his grandmother?"

"Yes, his parents have a nice condo in town somewhere, not sure where actually. I do know they have a home in I think Florida and also in the south of France. God, you don't think he's taken the girls out of the country?"

"No, it would be impossible without passports. The parents, what are their names?" Aaron said.

"The same, Carlos, he's a junior, Carlos the jerk that is, not the father. I think his mother's name is Mary. Virgin Mary, Carlos always called her, a very religious woman, I guess. I've never met her. Like I told them last night, I think he's been estranged from his parents for a while, but his mother sneaks him money from time to time."

Johnson and a couple of the other officers were writing things down.

"The only other name I recognize is this Arthur Goodwin. Isn't he the lawyer who did the plea bargain for Carlos? He had him sent to rehab instead of the work-house on that last aggravated assault charge, didn't he?"

That's correct. Mr. Goodwin is with the public defender's office and was the court-appointed attorney in the case you mentioned. We'll be talking to him first thing this morning."

I glanced over at the clock on the stove. It was only twenty minutes before seven. If Goodwin had any sense, he was still home in bed.

"Let me give you an update on what we have so far, which isn't much, but that doesn't mean it's necessarily all bad," Aaron said

A cloud seemed to cross over Isabella's face.

"Based on what we've learned up to this point, it would appear the girl's abduction was a spur of the moment incident. It may have been triggered by Mr. Haskell's appearance at the front door, or perhaps your not being home. Right now, we don't know. The positive side of this is that it means this was not a planned undertaking. What that suggests is there is an increased possibility that the girls will be released, possibly sooner rather than later. We are continuing our search and, in fact, redoubling our efforts. We have a statewide BOLO out for Carlos O'Kelly as well as your girls, and just to be on the safe side, we're extending that across a five-state region. I know it's difficult if not near impossible, but the best thing you can do for both yourself and especially for the girls is to remain calm and stay positive until we get them back. And, we will get them back."

Isabella nodded like she accepted the fact they were doing everything possible, which at the moment, other than rousting people out of bed in the middle of the night, wasn't much.

"Let's extend that BOLO to all the states en route to Florida. Find out the address of that Florida residence and contact local authorities and see if we can track down the parents of this idiot," Aaron said.

Isabella got up and walked into her bedroom then came back out a moment later. "I hoped like hell I'd never, ever have to use this again," she said and threw a faded yellow ribbon onto the table.

I'd seen it before. It had been tied to the tree out front when her husband Danny had been deployed. She'd kept it up for a few days after she got the word he'd been killed, but after the funeral, she'd asked me to take it down for her. I'd hoped like hell I'd never ever *see* the thing again.

# Five

Aaron and Officer Johnson remained at Isabella's for a while longer. By the time they were ready to go, there were easily a half dozen officers in the place monitoring the equipment set up to triangulate cellphone towers, tape calls, or God knows what.

It was all different from what we used to see in the old movies. Isabella was like the majority of the under fifty population living in the western world. She wasn't in the phone book, and she didn't have a landline.

As a matter of fact, one of the reasons she'd gotten a completely different cellphone number was because she had received a series of harassing phone calls from Carlos prior to his sentencing and entering rehab. The police were thinking her new phone number just might have been the event that precipitated his evening visit a little over twelve hours ago.

Aaron pulled me aside and said, "Hey, look, Dev, I'm about to take off. I could drop you down at Regions Hospital and let you get checked out. I can have someone standing by to give you a lift home once you get the okay. All you'll have to do is give me a call once the doc is finished checking you out."

"Thanks, but I'm okay, really," I said then hung on to the kitchen counter behind my back until things stopped spinning.

"I think you should get checked out, Dev, just as a precaution if nothing else. You took a couple of really hard hits to your thick skull. Even a little pea brain like yours is bound to be affected."

I shook my head slowly and made a mental note that I didn't feel like I was going to throw up when I did it, which I took as a small sign of improvement. "Thanks, but if you'd let me hop a ride and then if you could just drop me off at home, that would really help. Of course, I'd be forever in your debt. I just need to get cleaned up, change my clothes, plus I need to figure out what the hell I'm going to do for transportation until I get my car back from that bastard."

"I'd be happy to do that on one condition, Dev. All I ask is just one simple, little favor."

"Will you just relax, I already promised you I wouldn't get involved. How the hell would I even be able to do that, Aaron? Right now, in case you forgot, I'm on foot for Christ's sake. And just for the record, between my head throbbing and things spinning, I feel like I'm running at about fifty percent. All I want to do is rest up and get back to some semblance of normal."

"Whatever that is. Okay, I believe you, just as long as we understand one another. The last thing…."

"I got it, honest. You guys just bring those two little girls back home safe and sound."

I had my head tilted back, and my eyes closed for most of the ride home. I focused on keeping my stomach down every time Aaron rounded a curve or slowed to a stop, but thankfully the fireworks seemed to have stopped, at least for the moment. Neither one of us had spoken until Aaron turned onto Selby by the Cathedral. The huge bells were just in the process of chiming out the hour, and at first, I thought the sound was coming from inside my head.

"We get anything breaking on this, Dev, I'll let you know as soon as possible. Just remember your promise and stay away. That's the very best thing you can do to help bring this thing to a positive conclusion."

"For God's sake, Aaron, how the hell could I possibly forget? If you're not reminding me, you're threatening me every other time you say something. What part of 'I won't get involved' don't you believe?"

"I'd still like to get you down to the ER. Get that head looked at, I know you think it's getting better, but they might just pick something up on an x-ray."

"Yeah, and I'd like to get an hour-long back rub from Officer Patty along with some very personal attention from Officer Vang, but that ain't gonna happen either."

"Only 'cause there's a couple hundred guys in line ahead of you. If that's the way you're thinking, you're starting to come back around."

"Like I said, twenty-four hours will do a lot for my recovery. Besides, what if they give me an x-ray, and they find out I don't have a brain?"

"In that case, no one would be the least bit surprised. Anything comes to mind or happens on your end, Dev, you give me a call. I'll answer right away, I promise," he said, then pulled to a stop in front of my place and faced me. "Last chance, I can have you down at Regions Hospital in about four minutes."

"Thanks, but the first, in fact, the only priority is getting those two little girls back to Isabella. You just stay on the case and get this Carlos jackass off the streets before he does anymore damage."

"Then get the hell out of my car and let me get back to work," he smiled.

"Now it's my turn to say you look like shit and could use some rest."

"In time, Dev, all in good time."

# Six

I had a key to my front door hidden behind the drain pipe running down the side of the garage. Mercifully, I'd returned the thing to its hiding place after the last time I used it. I stepped in through my front door, took a deep breath, and thought it felt awfully damned good to be home and in familiar surroundings. That feeling lasted just about a nanosecond once I started to rehash all that had gone on since I had headed over to Isabella's yesterday just to watch her girls for a couple of hours. Things can change so quickly.

Right now, what I really needed was a long hot shower and then some serious sack time if I was going to be of any help to anyone.

I'd been standing in the shower for quite some time, just letting the water run over me and thinking. The water was hot, steaming, and it felt good to at least figuratively wash away recent events. I was extremely cautious with the bruising on my face. My head still hurt, but nothing like the throbbing I'd experienced last night. Still, I couldn't get those two little girls out of my mind. God help dip-shit Carlos if anything happened to those little angels, I'd hunt that bastard down to the ends of the earth and then take great pleasure inflicting all sorts of pain.

As I stood there thinking, I actually felt a slight chill, even though I was standing under the hot shower, and I thought that probably signaled it was time to just hit the sack and get some serious sleep. I turned the shower off and just stood while the water dripped off me for a brief moment, listening to the last of it gurgle down the drain. Then I pulled the shower curtain back.

"Oh, shit, it's just you. Here I was hoping to catch some beautiful babe. Looks like you could probably use a towel."

Fat Freddy Zimmermann grinned, then held out his hand and nodded at the towel bar on the far wall. One of two huge thugs wedged in the doorway smirked and then reached over, pulled a towel off the bar, and placed it in Freddy's hand. Freddy tossed the towel over to me.

He gave me the once over, moving his head up and down. "Hope you don't mind me saying so, but you really look like shit, Haskell."

"That seems to be a common perception. I think I've already heard that once or twice before today. Just what the hell are you guys doing in my bathroom? How in the hell did you even get into my house?"

"Fortunately for us, security apparently isn't your strong suit. The front door was unlocked, so we just thought this might be the perfect time to stop in and say 'hi.' Oh yeah, and Tubby would like the honor of your presence if you can fit it in, like right, fucking, now."

Tubby Gustafson represented the seamy underside of the saintly city. He was St. Paul's version of a home-grown crime boss. Grossly overweight, he was devious, a liar, politically connected, and a certifiable psychotic wacko. All of which were probably reasons why he and "Fat Freddy" got along so well.

Last I knew, Freddy had risen up in the ranks and was now serving as Tubby's enforcer. Although, given the size of the two Neanderthal muscle-bound thugs standing behind him, Freddy probably didn't have to get his hands too dirty on most days.

We had at least a passing working relationship, Freddy and I. He pretty much did whatever the hell he wanted, and I pretty much tried like hell to stay as far away as humanly possible.

"Mind if I put some clothes on?"

"I think we'd all prefer it if you did. By the way, what in the hell *did* happen to you? I wasn't kidding, Haskell, you really do look like shit. Another bout with the sidewalk, or did someone's husband come home early and take exception to you resting between his wife's thighs?"

"Something like that," I said, then took the towel from Freddy and began to dry my back.

"No offense, Haskell, but I think I'll just take a pass on your little show. I might just have to hightail it down-stairs to the kitchen and check things out. By the way, in case you've forgotten, Tubby doesn't like to be kept waiting. Why don't you two help Mister I-Forgot-to-

Duck, get dressed," he said to the two thugs as he exited the bathroom. I could hear the stairs creak as he made his way down to my kitchen, no doubt intending to raid my refrigerator.

"Who the hell do you expect to please with that little thing?" the thug leaning against the doorframe asked and pointed at me. Then the two of them laughed out loud at their fantastic sense of humor.

"Sorry, boys, I never liked whisker burn, so I guess you just wouldn't be my cup of tea. But, hey, who am I to object, whatever you two are into on your own time is none of my damned business."

They gave one another a confused look, then one of them growled, "Get your ass out here and get dressed, jerk-off."

My headache had returned to full throbbing force by the time we walked back to the kitchen. There were already a number of candy bar wrappers crumpled up on my kitchen counter next to the empty bag. Freddy held about a dozen Oreo cookies in his paw. He was chewing vigorously on the two or three he had already crammed into his mouth and looked ready to reload as soon as he swallowed.

"God," he said, spitting cookie crumbs across the kitchen counter. "Can't really say you look all that much better, but I guess it will just have to do. You know how Tubby is."

Unfortunately, I did know how Tubby was, and it wasn't doing much to improve my mood. "Can you tell me what this is about? Give me some idea what it is I was supposed to have done.”

“If you really want to know, I can give you at least a hundred thousand reasons. So if I were you, I’d start thinking pretty damned hard about how you plan to explain yourself. Come on, let’s go,” Freddy said, then snatched up what was left of my package of Oreo’s and waddled out of the kitchen to the front door.

# Seven

The ride to Tubby's private lunch time dining room was uneventful, as long as you didn't mind being crammed into the backseat of a Cadillac Escalade wedged between six hundred plus pounds of degenerate thuggery. Unfortunately, we seemed to make the drive in record time and quickly pulled into the No Parking zone along the curb. We screeched to a stop directly in front of the opulent double doors leading into The Derby, Tubby's exclusive restaurant.

The door on the righthand side had a piece of plywood over the area where the glass should have been. There were two guys working on the front doors. They were dressed in white overalls, short sleeve shirts with logos over the left breast, and white baseball caps that said Abbott Paint above the brim.

Toolboxes were scattered on the sidewalk, and it looked like they were getting ready to install a large glass panel in the righthand door. One of the guys was busily unscrewing a piece of plywood from the door. A set of sawhorses stood on the sidewalk with a beveled glass panel resting across it. Brown paper wrapped around the glass had been partially torn off and was blowing back and forth in the gentle breeze.

As we pulled along the curb, a thug leaning against the building straightened up then hurried over to open the car door for "Fat Freddy." As he oozed out of the front seat, the now empty, crumpled Oreo package he'd taken from my kitchen cabinet fell onto the sidewalk.

The workman with the drill stepped aside and gave Freddy a nod as he entered The Derby. I followed between the two Neanderthals, and the workman shook his head slightly when he looked at my battered face as if to say, "I wouldn't want to be in your shoes."

I felt that was a pretty accurate assessment.

The Derby's dim interior featured larger than life bronze-colored, plastic statues in a "Roman" motif positioned about every ten feet along the exterior walls. The statues, all naked women, held a bottle in one hand and a stemmed glass in the other. The figures were posed in various stages of toasting with the stemmed glass. Each statue had a black blindfold tied securely over her eyes. It seemed typical Tubby, vintage low class, and I tried not to contemplate any further images of Tubby's idea of restaurant debauchery.

A large bar ran across the length of the back wall with mirrors behind a series of shelves holding what looked like every liquor bottle known to man. Small blue lights ran along the length of each shelf, twinkling on and off and reflecting varying shades of blue off the massive array of bottles.

Six more blindfolded naked lady statues, arms extended over their heads, were arranged along the back of the bar and looked to be holding up a massive ceiling beam. Fake, long stem red roses were clasped in their mouths.

The room was dark, ostentatious to the point of being garish, and completely unoccupied with the exception of a large round table in the middle of the place draped with a white linen tablecloth. The table was illuminated by an overhead mirrored disco ball that spun round slowly, casting blue reflections out into the darkened recesses of the room, which did nothing to help my dizzy spell.

Tubby Gustafson sat at the table with a large linen napkin tucked beneath a couple of his chins. With the exception of a few wine dribbles, the napkin matched the table cloth hanging almost to the floor. He wore an off white sport coat with a red carnation stuffed into the buttonhole of his lapel.

A large steak platter was in front of Tubby with an even larger steak hanging over the sides of the platter. I guessed the steak to be about twenty-four ounces. Tubby gingerly cut a bite-sized piece with a sterling silver steak knife. He stabbed the piece of steak with his fork then held it up under the light of the disco ball for a closer examination before placing the steak in his mouth. He reached for a crystal wine glass that looked more like a large chalice, made a loud slurping sound, and then seemed to shudder in some form of orgasmic pleasure just as I was pushed into the light.

Tubby swallowed audibly. "What the— Haskell? Do tell. Is that really you?"

"Hello, Mr. Gustafson."

"If you don't mind my saying, you look like absolute shit. I'm trying to eat here, and now you wander in looking like that, might I suggest not exactly helping my appetite."

This brought chuckles and nods from the two heavies in dark suits sitting on either side of Tubby. He glanced left and right, acknowledging his own great sense of humor and maybe waiting for applause.

"And back so soon," he said, sloshing the crystal chalice to his lips and taking another giant slurp.

"Actually, I've never been in here before," I said cautiously moving my head around to indicate the darkened room.

"Really? I suppose you mean technically not *in* here. Isn't that right?"

"I've never been inside, and I've never been *here*, ever."

"You don't say. Hmmm-mmm, funny, must be our mistake then. You see, Haskell, early this morning, someone arrived here uninvited. He crashed one of my card games, Haskell. I don't mind saying he was rude, Haskell, very rude, not at all nice I might add. And if you can believe it, the bastard wore a mask, a Batman mask. I don't like Batman, Haskell."

"I'm sorry to hear that."

"Yes, I'm sure you are. You see, somehow this Batman character made his way in here with a gun, a big gun, wouldn't you say?" Tubby asked, then glanced at the jerks sitting on either side of him.

They nodded in agreement with Tubby, then turned and focused their attention on me with a cold, hard stare.

"Then, this Batman person waved this big gun around and pointed it at me. Can you believe that? My restaurant, my card game, with my friends, that son of a bitch isn't invited, and he points that big God damn gun right at me. As if that's not bad enough, he keeps it pointed at me until all the cash gets collected and passed up to my table. He even had a little pink suitcase with flowers on it to stuff the cash in. Then, this Bat-bastard backs out the door threatening to shoot anyone who follows. And, just to prove his point, before he left, he shot a bullet through my beveled glass window right out there, shattered the glass in one of the front doors to The Derby as a stupid warning."

"That doesn't sound like a very nice thing to do, but I'm not quite sure I'm following here, Mr. Gustafson."

"Hear that, he's not quite sure he's following," Tubby said to no one in particular. "Okay, Haskell, let me try and make it simple for you. Which way do you think Batman ran?"

"I, I really wouldn't have any idea, Mr. Gustafson. Really, I wouldn't know."

"I guess that would be reasonable. At least, that would sound reasonable if it weren't for one tiny little thing. You see, Haskell I like facts, incontrovertible facts," he said, then held out his righthand.

The jerk to his right reached into his suit coat. For a brief moment, I panicked and was afraid he might draw a gun. Instead, he pulled out a piece of folded notepaper and placed it in Tubby's hand.

"You seem to be a smart guy, so maybe you could help me out here, Haskell. I'd just like to get your input on this, seeing as how you're such a big-time investigator," Tubby said, unfolding the notepaper.

Both jerks smiled and seemed to chuckle to themselves.

"I wonder if, with that vast array of knowledge you seem to keep hidden from the rest of us if this might ring any bells in that thick skull of yours? A black Infiniti QX." Tubby glanced up at me and suddenly looked very pissed off. "A 2005 model with a rear taillight covered in red tape and a cracked windshield. Minnesota license FNL seven-four-nine. You tell me, Haskell, does that vehicle ring any bells up in that one-watt brain of yours?"

Yeah, alarm bells. "Well…"

"Guess who that vehicle turns out to be registered to?"

"It's mine, technically, sir. But, it was stolen last night, part of a kidnapping of two little girls. The guy who did the kidnapping, his name is Carlos. He assaulted me. Hell, you can see what he did to my face. Then, he kidnapped the two little girls I was babysitting."

"Really? And you expect me to believe that? Business must be slow, Haskell. Babysitting?"

"Honest Tubby, he—"

"You disgusting halfwit, you can't even tell a proper lie," he shouted. "Who in the hell would be crazy enough to trust you with children? Do you mean to tell me that this Bat-bastard kidnapped two little girls, then stole your car and since he then, no doubt had all sorts of time on his hands, the son-of-a-bitch waltzed into my card game last night, and put a gun to my head? Relieved me of close to a hundred grand and shot the window out of my front door?"

"Yes, sir, at least it kind of looks that way."

"Damn you," Tubby screamed, and suddenly, his crystal wine chalice sailed past my head, close enough that I heard it whistle and felt the breeze. It made a very distinctive, very expensive sounding tinkle when it smashed against the wall somewhere in the dark behind me. A fresh trail of red wine ran off across the white linen table cloth in my direction.

"I was probably being questioned by the police the whole time this must have been happening. After he stole my car, I had to get a ride home this morning from the police. I wasn't involved, Mr. Gustafson, I swear on a stack of Bibles, I really wasn't involved. I could have been unconscious for all I know. They even had the paramedics there to take care of me. If it's the same guy, this Carlos O'Kelly person, I only met him last night and then only for a few seconds, just long enough for him to assault me and knock me out. I swear I had nothing to do with this robbery, and I would never condone putting that gun to your head."

I noticed my hands had automatically folded together like I was pleading, which in a way probably wasn't too far from the truth. If I thought it would help my case, I would have gotten down on my knees.

"What was that name?"

"O'Kelly, Carlos O'Kelly."

Tubby looked at the jerks on either side of him. They looked at one another, and then both of them just shook their heads.

"Freddy?"

"Never heard of the guy."

"I can find out about him for you. I know up until maybe forty-eight hours ago he was in rehab, and I guess he just got tired of the straight life and basically walked away," I said.

"That's just what I need, you investigating for me. You're the whole reason I'm forced to even have this conversation. I'll find out about him, you just sit there in the dark and shut up, Haskell, so I don't have to think about you." Then he turned to the two jerks on either side of him and said, "Get on it."

The jerks stood, buttoned their suit coats before taking a moment to give me another glare, and then left the table.

"He's got curly—"

"Haskell, damn it," Tubby shouted. "Didn't I just tell you to sit in the dark and shut the fuck up? You're interrupting what's left of my meal, and I'd like to finish it in peace."

A small, bald waiter with a pencil-thin mustache and wearing a white coat suddenly stepped out of the darkness behind Tubby and placed a freshly-filled crystal chalice on the table in front of him.

"There, better, much, much better," he said. He made a show of carving the next bite of steak, stabbing the piece with his fork and holding it up to the light again for a brief examination before shoving the piece into his mouth.

# Eight

It was toward the end of Tubby's dessert course before the jerks hurried back from wherever they'd run off to. They placed a sheet of paper on the table in front of Tubby and next to what was left of a lemon meringue pie. Tubby was in the process of finishing his third piece.

"Mmm-hmm, no surprise, I figured as much," he grunted, then shoveled the final forkful of lemon meringue into his mouth and continued reading. When he had finished, he looked up and growled into the darkness, "Haskell, just where in the hell are you hiding?"

"Right here, exactly where you told me to sit and be quiet."

"Get into the light where I can see you, damn it."

Hands grabbed me from behind and shoved me into the circle of light surrounding Tubby's table.

"So, according to this shit…." Tubby nodded at the paper as he cut another giant piece of pie and placed it on his dessert plate. He scooped a massive piece off with his fork, opened wide, shoveled it in, and chewed a few times as if in contemplation. He talked with his mouth full, in the process spitting bits of lemon filling and meringue back out in my direction.

"It says here, this Carlos jackass was in for his third visit at Pleasant Lake Rehab when he just up and walked away. So much for the third time being a charm. Not to mention another thirty grand down the drain. Says here, the cops are looking for him for an assault, abduction, and kidnapping last night. And now I'm supposed to believe that's where you met him?"

"Yes sir. You see, I was the assault, and—"

"I don't recall asking you for an explanation, Haskell. I'm just trying to get to the facts. So, this bastard grabs the two little kids who were entrusted to you. Apparently, he throws them in your piece of shit car and then decides to swing by and ruin my night. Is that about right?"

"Not exactly, sir. He—"

"Haskell, for the record, I wasn't really asking for your opinion, so please just shut the hell up."

One of the jerks leaned over and whispered something into Tubby's ear, glaring at me as he did so.

"Yeah, that's right now that you mention it, excellent point, excellent," Tubby said. He took another giant forkful of pie, crammed it into his mouth, then gazed up into the disco ball, apparently attempting to think.

"Haskell, let me ask you another question. Now, I don't want an explanation. I just want a simple yes or no. Did you happen to have a gun in that horseshit car of yours?"

"Yes."

Tubby threw his fork onto his dessert plate. It bounced off the plate, sailed over what was left of the piece of pie, and shot toward me across the linen table cloth, leaving a lemon meringue skid mark about a foot long.

"You dumb shit, a, what the hell was it?" he asked the jerk who'd whispered to him a moment ago.

The jerk mumbled something to Tubby that I couldn't hear.

"A Sig Sauer? Was that what you kept in that piece of shit car of yours? A Sig Sauer?"

"Yeah, as a matter of fact." Wondering for just a nanosecond, how the thug next to Tubby would even know that.

"Well, surprise, surprise, surprise. Guess what, everybody? Amazingly, it all seems to come back to you, Haskell, another one of your grade A, major league screw-ups. And this time it's a really big screw-up, as a matter of fact it's a World Series screw-up."

"But I didn't—"

"For God's sake, will you ever shut up? Jesus wept. So let me get this straight, this O'Kelly douche bag links up with you, uses your car and by the way, borrows your gun to rob *me*. And, he kidnaps a couple of little girls in the process. That sound about right? Do I have that last part correct? For Christ's sake, even I think that is really low. A couple of God damned little kids. Just where in the hell does it end?"

I started to say something, but Tubby glared and turned beet red for a long moment, then he cut me off by slamming both fists down on the table, causing the plates and silverware to jump an inch or two.

"Shut up, shut up, shut up, damn it, will you please just once and for all shut-the-fuck-up, Haskell?"

I nodded and bit my lower lip.

"Alright, finally. Now, here's what's going to happen, Mister Private Investigator. I want those two little girls returned. I don't want to hear they're in your custody. I want them returned to someone responsible, like their mother. Then, you're going to get my money back from this Carlos friend of yours before I become the laughing stock of this city. This has the potential to be very bad for my business."

I started to say something, but Tubby just glared then turned to the jerks on either side of him and said, "This is the result of me being too patient. If he opens his mouth again, unless he's responding to a direct question from me, knock him out."

They both nodded and looked eager for the opportunity.

"Now, as I was just about to say. You are going to bring this Carlos bastard to me, do you hear? To me. I don't want to turn on the ten o'clock news and learn that he's been arrested and is burning up my tax dollars sitting on his fat ass in a comfortable damned jail cell somewhere or relaxing back in another posh rehab center. I want that shitty little piece of pond scum brought to me. You got that?"

"I hear you, Tub— err, Mister Gustafson, but, well, if you'll recall, I'm currently without a car, so it's going to be pretty difficult for me to find—"

"Does it ever end?" Tubby screamed then slurped more wine.

The thugs on either side of him got to their feet.

"No, no," Tubby said, indicating they should sit down. "I've had about all I can stand, Freddy, get this dunderhead a set of wheels, now. And, Haskell, only because I'm kind-hearted and in a forgiving mood, you've got forty-eight hours, that's it, got it? Freddy, get him the hell out of my sight before my generous side gives up in absolute disgust and simply stops working altogether. Jesus Christ."

A massive paw landed on my shoulder and pulled me out of the light from the disco ball and back into the darkness. Then, someone's foot kicked me in the ass and directed me toward the front door. The new beveled glass panel was already resting in the door, and one of the workmen was in the process of reinstalling the trim that held the thing in place.

Once we were out on the sidewalk, Freddy pulled me aside. He didn't seem to look all that happy. "God, you can sure screw things up. Here," he said and handed me the keys to the Escalade.

"Oh man, thanks, Freddy. I'm really not sure what to say. You're giving me your car?"

"You gotta be kidding me? You can't possibly be that stupid. What the hell do you think I am? No, I sure as hell am not giving you my car. I just want you to drive," he said, then waited while one of the thugs who served as his shadow opened the passenger door for him. "You two just wait here for me, I'll be back in a couple of minutes once I get dumb ass here set up."

Both thugs glared at me but didn't say anything as I hurried around to the driver's side and climbed behind the wheel.

# Nine

I buckled up and asked, "Where are we going?"
"Just head down West Seventh toward Otto, it's a stoplight. I'll tell you where to turn," Freddy said, then tilted his seat back and looked like he was getting ready to take a nap.

I headed down the street, passing a number of haunts, McGovern's, Moe's, Tommy Reeds, on and on it went. Leaning back in the seat with his eyes closed, Freddy looked like he was fast asleep, but about three blocks before Otto, he opened his eyes and said, "Take the next right."

I did that.

"You see that brick apartment building up there on the right? Just pull around in back and park."

I pulled into the alley running along the side of an apartment building, then into an asphalt parking lot behind the three-story beige brick structure. The lot was so small it was only marked off for four or five parking places, although I figured there had to be at least twenty-four units in the building.

"Let's go," Freddy groaned and unbuckled his seat belt before I'd even come to a stop.

I braked to a stop then got ready to put the car in reverse so I would be able to angle into one of the parking spots.

"What the hell do you think you're doing? Don't be wasting my time with that upstanding citizen shit, just park this damned thing. Tubby owns the damn building. God help anyone who hassles us."

I put the car back in drive, pulled across two of the parking places, stopped, and turned the car off.

"Better, much better, now, come on," Freddy said and climbed out of the car. He was at the back door of the building, pushing the button on the security system by the time I caught up to him.

The building looked like it had probably been built in the mid-fifties. A pattern of one large picture window, two medium windows, and a smaller bathroom window gave an indication of the apartment sizes. Based on the window layout, I figured probably eight units to a floor.

"Who the hell is it?" a groggy male voice growled out of the speaker after Freddy pressed the buzzer a half dozen times.

"Open the damned door, numbnuts, its Freddy."

"Freddy?"

Freddy gave me a look that suggested, *what's with everyone today*, and shouted, "Just open the damn door."

A buzzer rasped a moment later, and I heard the lock click. Freddy pushed the door open and walked in. "Give me those car keys so I can get the hell out of this joint.

God, I hate this place, come on, he's upstairs," he groaned then headed up a flight of grimy stairs.

We climbed up the stairs to the third floor. The air seemed to grow noticeably worse with each floor. The stairwell walls probably hadn't been repainted since the place was built somewhere back in the early Eisenhower administration. A two-foot-wide patch of grime ran along the walls from over sixty years of grubby hands being rubbed along them.

By the time we made it up to the third floor, Freddy was red-faced and breathing heavily.

"Jesus, I don't know how he does it every day. It's enough to give you a heart attack. Must be the thin air," Freddy mumbled.

The hallway reeked of something not very pleasant, and I noticed two white trash bags sitting at the far end of the hall. One of the bags had a long slit on one side and what was left of a stuffed chicken, or maybe it was just a rat, had fallen out, and piled up onto the soiled hallway carpet. Unfortunately, we headed in that direction, the smell of something very rotten grew stronger with every step we took. Freddy stopped at the door next to the trash bags and tried the knob.

"Open the damned door, asswipe," Freddy screamed then pounded on the door. The doorway across the hall opened, but then quickly closed as soon as the woman looked out and saw who was making the racket. Freddy glared across the hall for a brief moment then pounded on the door again just as it opened.

A thin, bald guy with wispy grey hair pulled back in a ponytail, a sparse grey beard and sunken eyes stood in front of us. He was wearing a strappy T-shirt that needed a serious washing and was in the process of zipping up the fly on his jeans. He had an Adam's apple about the size of the doorknob and looked like he weighed no more than a hundred-and-thirty pounds soaking wet.

"Got me waiting out here in the hall smelling your shit, come on, man, I got things to do, I ain't got all day," Freddy said then barged past the guy and into the apartment, I followed in his wake. Things in the apartment didn't smell much better than the hallway.

The kitchen area off to the left was littered with dirty plates and dishes. A half-eaten plate of fried eggs with a cigarette stuck dead center into one of the yolks sat on a small table surrounded by beer bottles and empty glasses.

A rather unattractive woman with mousey hair, sharp features, and a hook nose sat on a threadbare couch. She looked like she outweighed numb nuts by at least a hundred pounds and was in the process of lighting a cigarette.

She didn't bother to introduce herself, say hello or wave, but just blew a cloud of smoke up toward the ceiling then wiggled into the corner of the couch not bothering to close the red nylon robe she wore. The coffee table in front of her was littered with a bong, a number of plastic bags that looked like they'd once held dope, a couple of overflowing ashtrays, and more empty beer bottles.

"That there's, Rachel," numbnuts said giving a nod toward the exposed woman on the couch. Then he gave me the once over and said, "Man, you look like shit. What the hell happened?" he asked Freddy.

Freddy just shook his head and said, "Never mind. He's gonna need the keys to your car."

"What? My car? You gotta be kidding me."

"Do I sound like I'm kidding, give him your damn keys."

"No way, come on, man. It's a classic, and I'm thinking about maybe restoring it. And you want me to just hand the keys over to this piece of shit. I got news for you, he ain't getting anywhere near…."

"Is there a problem here? Did you just hear what the hell I said? I told you to give him your car keys, numb-nuts."

"But Freddy, how in the hell am I supposed to get around? I got shit happening, man. I got people to see, places to go, you know. I got appointments and shit, I can't just turn that vehicle over to this worthless piece of shit, it's a vintage collectors car."

"Give him the keys now before I start to lose it."

"Freddy, come on, please. You can't do this to me, man. Tell you what," he leaned in closer to Freddy and whispered. "You see Rachel over there. She'd really dig showing you a thing or two. I could line it up for you, take her, hell go ahead and use my room, be my guest, Freddy, on the house."

Freddy reached under his jacket and pulled out a small pistol. Then he racked a round into the chamber and started shaking his head. His face flushed, and he shoved the pistol into the guy's ribs.

"Does anyone ever fucking listen anymore," Freddy screamed. Then he glared and hissed, "I'm not kidding here, numbnuts, give him your car keys, now or I'm going to really lose it. It's already been a very long day for me."

"But, Freddy."

Freddy backhanded him with the pistol across the side of his forehead, and the guy went down, knocking a floor lamp onto the coffee table in the process. Then he placed a foot on either side of the guy groaning on the carpet, rolled him over, and pressed the pistol onto the end of his nose.

"Last time, numbnuts. Give me the keys, now, before I blow your brains out all over the carpet, and then you won't get your damage deposit back. You understand?" he said almost in a whisper.

"Okay, okay, Jesus, just take it easy, dude, take it easy," he half whimpered as he hurriedly dug into his jean pockets. He pulled out a set of keys and handed them to Freddy. "There, okay, you got 'em, hope you're happy, man."

Freddy snatched the keys then seemed to sigh as he stood up, he took a deep breath, stuffed the pistol back under his jacket and seemed to calm down. "Better, much, much better."

He handed me the keys and indicated the door with a nod of his head. As I opened the door, Freddy said, "Nice to meet you, Rachel, maybe some other time." And we walked out.

We could hear Rachel yelling once we were out in the hall and until we were halfway down the stairs. "You dumb shit. Now how in the hell am I supposed to get home? I knew getting together with you wasn't going to work out for me, everyone warned me, but oh no…."

Freddy walked out the back door to the Escalade and said, "His bomb is out there on the street, in front of the building, the thing is painted blue, you can't miss it. If I were you, I'd kind of get my ass in gear. I don't think Tubby was kidding. You got about forty-eight hours to find this guy and return that money, or we'll have to come looking for you. I'd just as soon not have to do that."

# Ten

Freddy was right, the car was a bomb and painted iridescent blue where it wasn't rusted. The thing was impossible to miss. A 1960, two-door, Cadillac Biarritz parked on the street in front of the building and just about the size of an aircraft carrier. It sat there wheezing alongside the curb, pointed in the wrong direction with a couple of parking tickets slipped beneath the windshield wiper.

It was a convertible, with the top up, although the back of the top was torn almost all the way across, and the rear window was missing. I peeked through the grimy side window and saw that the rear seat was gone as well. In place of the seat, a small mattress, without a sheet, had been crammed in the space with what looked like black hosiery attached to all four corners of the mattress. The hosiery appeared to have been used as a restraint, and I tried not to contemplate the various options.

I slipped behind the wheel and prayed the thing would start. I noticed an empty half-pint bottle of peppermint schnapps hanging out beneath the driver's seat when I settled in. I opened my door and tossed the bottle onto the boulevard then wiped my hand off on my jeans.

When I turned the key, the ignition seemed to groan for a long moment, and just when I thought *Oh God*, it fired up with a throaty roar and a black cloud of sooty exhaust rolled down the street. I checked the mirrors, then pulled away from the curb and headed back over to Isabella's.

Given its size, the car actually handled pretty well on the road, although the flapping noise from the torn top and the continual cloud of exhaust were a bit worrisome. I pulled in front of Isabella's, and after the third attempt, I managed to parallel-park the car between two others.

Autumn leaves were just beginning to fall partially covering the street and the little front lawns. I noticed what looked like three unmarked police cars scattered along the block and one squad car with a cop sitting be-hind the wheel. He climbed out of his car and stood in the middle of the street, looking bored while I took my time parking.

When I turned off the car he gave me a signal with his hand to roll down the window. "Can I help you, Sir," he asked, then gave a long, uneasy stare at the bruises on my face.

"I'm here to see Isabella. I was here yesterday."

"Could I see some identification, please?" he said, then looked back and forth along the length of the car like he couldn't quite believe what he was seeing. By this time, the cloud of exhaust had drifted across the street and was slowly dissipating.

I handed him my wallet.

"If you wouldn't mind taking your license out of your wallet, please."

I did as instructed and handed the license to him.

"Please wait right here, this shouldn't take more than a minute or two," he said then walked back to his squad car.

I could see him first on the radio, then on a cellphone. It was more like a good five minutes before he walked back, handed me my license, and said, "You can go in. Sorry, we have to check everyone who goes in or out, just to play it safe. They may check you again at the front door."

"Have there been a lot of visitors?"

"Actually, you're the first, other than some news folks, and they don't really count. We're supposed to keep them away, and once they've cooled their heels out here for an hour or two, they usually head off to some other story. Mind me asking what kind of mileage you get with this thing?"

"I can usually make it to the next gas station, as long as I keep an eye on it. I think I'm getting about nine miles to the gallon," I lied. "Not what you'd call the most fuel efficient."

"You gonna restore it?"

"I'm thinking about it, but it might be a little more work than I want to take on right now."

He nodded, then stepped back and scanned along the length of the thing one more time. "You'd need to find two parking spaces wherever you go.  It was a different world back then," he said and shook his head.

I noticed three guys drinking coffee and staring at me from Isabella's living room window as I made my way up the front sidewalk. The faded yellow ribbon was tied around the maple tree in the front yard. One of the coffee drinkers opened the front door before I had the chance to ring the doorbell then stood there, blocking the entrance just staring at my face.

I handed him my driver's license before he had a chance to say anything.

"You're Haskell?" he asked and then gave a closer examination to my face before looking back at my license.

"Yeah, here to see Isabella."

"Man, he did a job on you, better come on in," he said, pulled the door open, and stepped back.

Isabella was on the living room couch sitting in front of the TV. I noticed my empty beer bottle from last night was still on the carpet alongside the couch. I don't think she was watching or even hearing whatever was playing on the tube. She looked exhausted and understandably stressed out. The always perfectly put together person, that I knew had limp, unkempt hair, and wore the same clothes that she'd had on the day before only now more wrinkled and disheveled like she'd slept in them, which she most likely had. Her hair hadn't been combed, and her face was devoid of makeup. The mascara that had run beneath her eyes and down her cheeks last night had been removed. In its place were deep, dark circles surrounding red, puffy eyes.

She gave me a half nod and said, "Hey."

There was obviously no use in asking if she'd heard anything, but I asked anyway. "Any news?"

She just shook her head and went back to staring at the TV, after a long moment she said, "There's some coffee in the kitchen, I think." She indicated the kitchen with a slight nod of her head and returned to staring blankly at the flat screen.

I walked out to the kitchen. A guy in shirt sleeves with a crewcut was seated at the counter, working a crossword puzzle in the newspaper.

"What's another word for oatmeal?"

I thought for a minute then said, "Try porridge."

He penned that in and sat back for half a moment, looking satisfied. "Yeah, that works, thanks. Hey, coffee's over there," he said, indicating the coffeemaker next to the kitchen sink. Then he gave me a slight nod and went back to his crossword and started chewing on the end of his pen.

I emptied the pot and got barely half a mug. From the taste of the coffee, it must have been on since last night. I turned off the coffee maker, took another sip, then set my mug in the sink, figuring I was better off without the stuff. I stepped alongside the genius with the crossword puzzle.

"Any idea what state is the "First in Flight?"

"Try North Carolina," I said.

He penned it in and gave another satisfied look,

"Has there been any news?" I asked, keeping my voice down.

He didn't bother to look up, but shook his head and said, "No nothing. Not so much as a wrong number."

"Any idea where he could be?"

He slowly looked up at me and focused for the first time then said, "I guess if we had an idea, we'd probably be there. What the hell happened to you?"

"I'm the guy he coldcocked last night."

He nodded and went back to his crossword.

I walked back out to the living room. I watched Isabella wring her hands for thirty minutes, then drifted back to the dining area and asked the three guys who'd been staring out the window earlier if there was any news.

"Not a damned thing," one of them half-whispered then looked out toward Isabella, staring blankly at the TV. "Kind of strange actually. We're thinking he might be out of state, probably heading south or maybe making a beeline out to California and the wine country."

"That's gonna bring the Fed's in," said the only one of the three still wearing his sport coat.

Just then, the crewcut from the kitchen got up from his crossword puzzle and came out to join us. "They're already on their way, the Feds. I just got the call. They'll be here in the next half hour."

"Maybe they'll have some new information, a sighting, God forbid a clue or something," someone said.

"That would be nice, but my guess is they'll show up with the same thing we got, nothing."

I waited around, cooling my heels until the FBI showed up. There were just two of them, in starched white shirts and dark suits. Introductions were made, I shook hands with the one in the grey suit and immediately forgot his name. Agent Osborne wore a blue suit.

"Haskell, you're the one O'Kelly assaulted, right?" Osborne asked and then zeroed in on my battered face.

"Yeah, that's me."

"By the looks of things, he nailed you pretty good, no offense, but you look like shit."

"Thanks. You have anything new on this guy? A sighting, a phone call, some bizarre history?" I asked.

"Well, with all due respect, that information is frankly on a need to know basis, and I'm not sure you're exactly in the loop. When something of merit comes up, we'll make a statement to the proper sources and you can get the information just like everyone else," Osborne said then glanced around at the group as if to say, "I'm in charge, now."

"So, in other words, you know as little as anyone else, which is just one big fat nothing."

Osborne gave me a look like he was about to say something, but the guy with the crewcut spoke first.

"I think under the circumstances, Mr. Haskell could be privy to some general information. It might just prompt something he forgot to mention."

Osborne seemed to consider this for a moment then said, "Okay, your man was in rehab until about forty-eight hours ago. No cellphone we know of, no familiar haunts, no friends he's been with. Bit of a shadowy character here, so we're dealing with a pretty blank slate. Doesn't seem to have accomplished very much thus far in his life."

"You think he's left the state?"

"I'd say it's highly probable, the behavior at this stage would seem to suggest that's a good possibility."

"What behavior?"

"The fact that he hasn't made any contact suggests he's most likely in the flight mode. It would be a typical response."

"Typical response?"

"Yes, an attempt to distance himself from the entire incident, in both a physical as well as a mental way."

I waited to hear about the visit Carlos paid to Tubby's card game, but no one mentioned it. Now I was pretty sure both the cops and the FBI didn't have the slightest idea. A hundred grand could go a long way toward travel expenses. Old Carlos could have flown down to South America or out to Hawaii for that matter.

I was pretty sure of one thing, if I mentioned the card game, they'd immediately corner Tubby, and then Tubby would cancel my forty-eight-hour reprieve and just have me killed.

"Maybe he's just sitting somewhere drinking Pina Coladas and watching the kids play on the beach," I said.

Osborne gave me a look and said, "If you'll maybe wait in the next room, I'd like to begin working our response here." Then he turned his attention to the local cops.

I wasted the better part of another hour twiddling my thumbs and accomplishing absolutely nothing. Eventually, I made my exit feigning a doctor's appointment. Based on the way I looked, no one questioned me.

The initial stages of the turf war between the city's finest and Agent Osborne were just beginning to simmer as I headed for the front door. Osborne was in the process of taking charge, and the locals didn't look very happy.

I gave Isabella a hug and kiss on my way out the door. Understandably, she seemed numb to the world and didn't react at first. Then she grabbed my hand just as I began to step away. She looked up at me from the couch as tears welled up in her red, puffy eyes, and she whispered, "Dev, he isn't going to call. I need my babies back. You've got to find them for me."

I nodded, tried to step away, but she squeezed my hand even tighter and pulled me toward her. "Maybe you didn't hear me, I mean it, Dev. My babies, you have to find them. Promise me."

"The police...."

"Find them, damn it, find them, promise me," she whispered.

"I'll try and find them. I promise I'll try."

She let go of my hand and just stared at the floor. The feds and the local guys were arguing around the dining room table and didn't seem to notice the two of us. I bent down and kissed her on the top of the head and whispered again, "I promise."

The cop sitting in the squad car looked up from the magazine he'd been reading and watched me navigate the car back and forth a half dozen times until I was able to edge into the street. Then he gave me a slight nod as I rumbled past and returned to his magazine.

I had no idea where to begin.

# Eleven

My cell rang not too long after I left Isabella's. I was behind the wheel barreling down the interstate. I gave a quick glance, but couldn't recognize the number. I could hear a voice, but between the torn top flapping in the wind and the rumbling exhaust belching a cloud of noxious black soot as I barreled down the road, I couldn't make out what was said. A smarter guy would have probably just pulled over and listened.

"I'm sorry, could you talk a little louder, it must be the connection, I'm still having trouble hearing you."

"Hey, listen up, dip-shit, I just said, did you find that idiot and get our money back yet?"

"Freddy?"

"The one and only. So what's the news, when can we expect to see you with that suitcase?"

"Freddy, it's been about thirty seconds since I got behind the wheel of this bomb. So, no, I have not been able to retrieve Tubby's money. I've barely been able to begin looking."

"Retrieve, I like that, a fancy college word, retrieve, yeah I'm gonna file that and use it sometime. That's classy, Haskell, really classy. You know, if I didn't know any better…."

"Is there a purpose to this call?"

"Take it easy, bitch, just trying to help you out, man. Maybe lend a little assistance to your search for this Carlos dildo. You might wanna think about being just a little nicer to the only friend you got out there."

"Help me out?"

"Yeah, actually, I think we got a sighting."

"A sighting? Of Carlos?"

"No, we got a sighting of Angelina Jolie and Brad Pitt, and I figured you'd want to be the first to know. Jesus, yeah, your buddy Carlos. Why the hell else would I waste my time calling you?"

"You're kidding? Let me guess, that dumb shit is either heading toward Chicago or he's maybe on his way out to California, right?"

"Chicago? What makes you say that? He may be stupid, but not that stupid. Why the hell would he go down there?"

"Oh, so it is California."

"The same question, why in the hell would he want to drive all the way out there, that sounds really half-ass. And you do this for a living? Where do you come up with this kind of shit?"

"The cops seem to think he's heading out of town, in fact, they made a point of saying out of state, actually."

"That'll bring the Feds in."

"I got news for you. They're already here."

"No shit? Hey, hold on, you didn't happen to mention his appearance at The Derby last night, did you? They get word of that and, well, it ain't gonna be a very pretty picture. So it would be wise to just keep your mouth shut on that subject."

"I'm not that stupid, Freddy."

"Oh, really? 'Cause you sure had me fooled. The Feds already on the scene brings on a lot more pressure. I suppose they're looking for the kids and don't have the foggiest idea this clown is running around with a hundred-grand of Tubby's hard earned dough."

"I'm guessing you're right. To tell the truth, I don't have much to go on right now, I don't even know where this guy lives."

"Well, that just means you better be getting your ass in gear."

"You said you saw him?"

"Not me, we got word a little while ago he was seen up at the Lumberyard. Does that mean anything to you?"

"The Lumberyard? What the hell would he be doing there? You mean like where you buy….?"

"No, not a place like that, he ain't building a house or anything. The Lumberyard, dumb shit, it's a strip club. Tubby owns the joint it's up in the northern suburbs, just outside of Big Lake."

"Big Lake?"

"Yeah, you know it?"

"Kind of, and this joint's called the Lumberyard?"

"That's what I just got done telling you. Yeah, apparently your boy Carlos was up there about midnight last night, got the car on their security tape and everything. You should get your ass up there and talk to a guy named Leroy. He's got the security tape and maybe some other information. Tubby told him to stay put until you talked to him and watched the tape."

"I'm on my way now. Freddy, you got a phone number you can give me for that place?"

"I'll text it to you, so you're not writing it down while you're driving. You know how to read a text, don't you?"

I made my way across town, then hopped on 35W and took that up to Highway 10. With the rush hour starting to build, it took about an hour-and-a-half of bumper-to-bumper traffic before I was on the outskirts of Big Lake.

I'd probably been through the town once or twice, but I couldn't remember when the last time was. Highway 10 is the main drag through town, and I drove past a lake although it didn't look all that big. Just beyond what passed for the downtown area, a large billboard advertised "The Lumberyard two miles ahead."

The place turned out to be a one-story, cinder block building that looked suspiciously like it might have originally been built as a grocery store. The only lumber I could see were sheets of plywood covering up the windows. The plywood was painted in bright red and yellow letters saying *'Girls, Girls, Girls.'*

The building sat right next to the Central Methodist church, and it looked like the two operations shared parking lots. I guess you had to sin before you could be saved.

I pulled the car into two spaces next to a plumber's panel truck and listened to the engine cough and sputter for the next thirty seconds before it finally stopped. Then I waited while my hearing slowly returned after listening to the torn top flap for the last sixty miles.

I called the number Freddy had sent me. Leroy answered after a half dozen rings.

"Yeah."

"Leroy?"

"Who the hell did you expect?"

"Fat Freddy gave me this number, said you got images of a guy we're looking for on your security tape."

"Oh, you, it's about damned time, man. I just wanna let you know I've wasted the whole damned day waiting for your ass to show up. When in the hell are you headed up here?"

"I'm in your parking lot."

"Jesus, finally, something's going my way. Just hustle your ass in here, you can ask one of the bartenders for me, and they'll point you in the right direction. And don't even think about stopping for a beer or watching the girls."

Charming.

The bartender I talked to wore a pasted-on smile and a skimpy black negligee. She removed the smile as soon as I asked directions to Leroy.

"So, you don't want a beer, which means I ain't gonna get a tip, ain't that just perfect. Hey, man, no offense, but you kinda look like shit. That hurt?" she asked, giving my face the once over.

"Just point me toward Leroy, okay."

"Whoa, dial down, baby. No need to get all worked up. You see that door over there next to the stage?"

I turned around and peered across the darkened room to a distant door labeled 'PRIVATE.' "The one with the red light above it?"

"Yeah, good guess, of course, that's also the only door over there. Anyway, just go in that door. His office is at the end of the hall. It's the door labeled 'asshole,' you can't miss him."

There were maybe a dozen folks in the place, virtually all guys at no surprise. Well, except for the woman gyrating up and down against a chrome pole. None of the patrons seemed to be paying any attention to her. She grabbed the pole and spun around on the thing a couple of times before she slowed to a stop and looked even more bored than when she started. More than a few heads turned to look at me as I made my way past empty tables toward the far side of the room.

A fat guy with a shaved head was leaning against the wall next to the door. He was standing on one foot with the other braced against the wall. His arms were folded, and he seemed even more bored than the woman on stage. It was tough to tell in the dim light, but he almost looked like he was asleep.

He was dressed all in black; T-shirt, jeans, boots, and a baseball cap. His T-shirt didn't quite cover his beer-belly, and he flashed about a four-inch-wide strip of hairy skin and navel. As I reached for the doorknob, he oozed over against the door, so it wouldn't open.

"Can's back over there on the far side of the room, next to the bar, pal. Or you can take it outside and use the parking lot. I don't care. But, this here's a private entrance, just for the talent."

"Talent?" I said. "I'm supposed to see Leroy. He's waiting for me."

"You the bastard he's been bitching about for the last couple of hours? God, we've all had to listen to him, he's put everyone in the place on a downer, man. You're the one he's been waiting for, right?"

"Probably."

"Good luck, man," he said, then studied my face for a moment. "Looks like things ain't exactly gone your way today, either. Don't mind me saying, but you kinda look like shit, dude." Then he drifted back against the wall, took up his position, and pasted the bored look back on his face.

# Twelve

The hallway was painted industrial olive drab, had dim yellow lights that flickered and reeked of cheap perfume. I walked past a door with "Dresing Room" written in black marker. Apparently, spelling wasn't a priority at the Lumberyard. Leroy's door was at the end of the hall with a plastic sign on it that read "Knock." Someone had added an "ers" next to the plastic sign so that it read "Knockers."

"Get the hell in here," a voice shouted after I knocked. He growled as I opened the door. "About God damn time. I got a life too, you know," he said, then focused on me for a long moment. "No offense, but Jesus, you look like shit, what the hell happened to you?"

"It's one of the reasons I'm here."

My looking like shit seemed to be a common theme currently playing across the upper Midwest. I couldn't disagree, but in my case, it was a temporary situation. Leroy, on the other hand, was a permanently rather unpleasant looking man with bulging, bloodshot eyes, a nose that looked like a bratwurst with acne and a three-day beard. He took a sip from a drink. Based on the color, I guessed it to be either bourbon or Scotch, then he gave a satisfied little gasp exposing a triangular-shaped gap between his yellowed front teeth. I figured the gap was most likely the result of some differing opinions.

A half dozen security monitors with black and white images were mounted on the wall behind him. Two of the monitors appeared to cover the inside of the bar, two covered the exterior of the building, and one covered what appeared to be the inside of the dancers' dressing room where two women were currently applying makeup in front of a large mirror.

The final monitor had a frozen image of my car. I could tell it was my Infiniti QX because you could see the crack along the passenger side of the windshield, and just in case I still had any doubts, the front license plate was clearly visible.

"You got a tape I guess I'm supposed to see?"

"Yeah, yeah, I've had this damned thing cued up and sitting here for the better part of the day, just waiting here for you to finally show up, not to mention me wasting the entire day. I been sitting here ever since we got the word from Tubby."

"Got the word?"

"I suspect he alerted every business in the organization, looking for that damned car and this fool." He said then spun around on his squeaky desk chair. He clicked a couple of keys on a keyboard resting in front of the screen, and the image immediately sprang to life.

It was a jerky feed and in black and white. I guessed an image maybe every four or five seconds. At first, the only motion was some headlights going down the road in the background. Then suddenly jackass Carlos appeared in shirtsleeves carrying a large glass of what appeared to be a pretty fancy drink. It looked like there was a little parasol stuffed into one side of the glass. He seemed to turn and say something, then suddenly a woman slinked across the screen.

She had white-blonde hair, cut short on the sides with bangs. She was wearing a pair of what looked like clear plastic heels, skyscraper heels, maybe a thong, and a jacket that hung open and wasn't doing a very good job of covering her. The more I studied the jacket, the more I thought it looked an awful lot like my missing bomber jacket.

She was carrying a large drink as well. She held the glass with both hands while Carlos took a big sip from it, then he evidently said something that got her laughing. She took another large sip, then staggered around to the passenger side of the car and climbed in.

As Carlos fired up my car, you could see the woman turn and peer into the backseat. She seemed to be laughing and took another large pull on her drink while Carlos said something back. Then she hit Carlos on the shoulder, but in a playful manner. Carlos turned the headlights on, and they drove out of sight.

"What time was that?"

"Little after midnight," Leroy said, then clicked a couple of keys, and a digital readout popped up in the lower right corner of the screen. "Thirty-seven minutes after midnight to be exact."

"Run it for me again."

Leroy sighed with the effort of having to click three or four keys on the keyboard. The image of my car appeared, and I watched as the tape replayed. I couldn't be sure, but I was willing to guess that when the blonde looked into the backseat of my car, she saw the girls, probably asleep. And for whatever reason, she thought that was something worth laughing about.

"You know who that woman is?"

"Name's Rikki."

"Rikki?"

"Yep. Like Rikki Martinez, only this one ain't famous.

"She a regular?"

"She dances here from time to time. Bit of a loner, I guess you could say. Hell, they're all screwed up in one way or another. From what I can pick up, none of the other girls seem to know that much about her. Likes her vodka. Never seems to cause any real problems, far as I know."

"You see the guy in here before?"

"No, which ain't all that unusual, 'specially this time of year."

I gave him a look suggesting I wasn't quite following.

"It's hunting season for the next three months, one thing or another. Got your pheasants, ducks, geese, deer, bear, wolves now...."

"I get it."

"It's Minnesota, man."

"But you don't recall him being in here before."

"Not that I can remember."

"So how'd he pick her up so fast?"

"Your boy there was dropping some pretty heavy tips, place like this it don't take long for him to catch every girl's attention. It's probably just a case of Rikki being the first one to offer a little bit more value for the dollar," Leroy said, then smiled at his own attempt at humor.

"You got shots of him inside?"

"Yeah, I can get 'em up if you really want to take a look. Not that much to see, I suppose he was here for maybe an hour, tops. No longer than that. You'll see, she glams onto him real quick like."

"Let me see him inside."

That brought another long sigh, and Leroy suffered through clicking a few more keys. Carlos suddenly appeared behind a large, snifter-shaped glass with a paper umbrella stuck along one side. He took a couple of hearty gulps and drained the glass to the halfway point before he set the umbrella on the table. He casually glanced around but didn't appear to be worried or anxious.

A dark-haired woman in a thong walked up to him and said something in his ear, he shook his head and apparently waved her off. Rikki suddenly drifted in front of him a half minute later. They seemed to chat for a long moment, then she pushed him back in his chair, straddled him, and proceeded to rub his head between her breasts. Carlos said something, and she leaned back and nodded. He nodded back, and she gave him a three or four-minute lap dance.

Carlos looked to be enjoying the activity, and Rikki, staring over his shoulder, looked bored. Eventually, she finished, pulled a chair up next to him, and they started talking.

A moment later she ordered a drink, gesturing with her hands and giggling, Carlos gave the waitress a nod. Once the drinks arrived, Rikki leaned over and whispered something in his ear. It wasn't more than thirty seconds later, Rikki donned my bomber jacket, picked up her king-sized drink, and the two of them headed for the door.

"What about this Rikki, chick? I don't suppose there's any chance you'd have an address for her?"

"Figured you'd ask that I'm way ahead of you," he said and pushed an envelope across his desk.

I opened it up and pulled out a sheet of paper with a handwritten address and phone number as well as her social security number, all of it nice and neat. Leroy's name and number were written at the bottom of the sheet.

"Kare Phree?" I said, reading the address. "What the hell is that? It sounds like some sleazy retirement community."

"It's a park."

"A park?"

"Yeah, you know, mobile homes, bums, your general malcontents, a *trailer* park. It's just about five miles west of town." Leroy said, then proceeded to give me detailed directions. I wrote them down on the paper.

"Okay," I said, folding the paper and slipping it into a back pocket.

"Anything else?" he asked.

"No, this is great, appreciate the help."

"You be sure to tell old Tubby I was a big help."

"I'll be sure to do that, Leroy."

"Good, now get the hell out of here. I need to get home and do some of the things I've been waiting on all damned day."

# Thirteen

The Kare Phree trailer park looked about as appealing as its name, not very. The sign at the entrance consisted of a four-by-four sheet of half-inch plywood painted with flaking white paint and the words Kare Phree stenciled in twelve-inch black letters. A large red arrow below the letters pointed toward the entrance.

The lower-left corner of the sign looked like some rabid dog had bitten it off. Weeds, maybe three feet high, effectively hid the lower half of the sign. There was an outdoor light attached to the top of the sign, but either the bulb had burned out, or no one had bothered to turn the light on.

Against my better judgment, I followed the red arrow and entered the Kare Phree trailer park. The streets, if you could call them that, were little more than rutted dirt trails, winding off in different directions. Each seemed to be named after a president though not laid out in any apparent order. Rikki's trailer was number 415 and sat somewhere on Madison Lane.

The deep ruts and the occasional pothole or massive tree root made any thought of speeding an impossibility.

As I eased through the place, I noticed more than one car up on blocks, bicycle frames missing wheels and seats, the occasional discarded mattress, and lots of broken pieces of furniture. Haphazard screened porches in various states of disrepair seemed to be tacked onto every other place. Rust appeared to be the common denominator among the trailers.

I ventured deeper into the maze. More than a few large dogs barked, bared their teeth and strained at the ropes holding them in place. With all the trash bags piled up around the place, one could only hope tomorrow was the collection day.

As I turned onto Madison, I drove through a swarm of plastic wrappers blowing across the ruts in the road. A rusty mailbox numbered 415 was mounted on a weathered post leaning at an angle.

Rikki's place looked awfully dark, and the single car parking area alongside her trailer sat empty. I pulled into the parking place as best I could, but the car still hung out into the rutted trail by a good five or six feet. Someone's rabid dog continued to bark nonstop from a trailer nearby.

I took out the piece of paper with Leroy's notes and dialed the number he'd written down for Rikki.

A recording clicked in after the first ring. "The number you have reached is temporarily not in service." Meaning, her phone had been disconnected. That was disappointing, but from the very little I knew about her, not really a surprise.

I gave a quick look around before I opened her mailbox. There were a number of envelopes along with at least a dozen grocery store circulars. I grabbed the envelopes and quickly fanned through them. A cable bill, two cellphone bills, and a couple of past-due notices were interspersed with pre-approved credit card offers and, a postcard from St. Louis signed Eric.

I opened up the past due notices. One was from the power company, which might explain the no lights. The second was from a credit card company stating that privileges had been revoked and would be reinstated just as soon as the bill for three-hundred-and-thirty-nine bucks was brought current. A third notice was from her bank, alerting her to an overdraft for sixty-one dollars.

I brought the envelopes up to the door. The front stoop consisted of six cinderblocks lying unevenly on their side. There was an aluminum screen door, but the door handle, the window, and for that matter, the screen were all missing. I knocked on the storm door and waited.

The wooden storm door was a cheap, hollow-core thing with a wood veneer that was warped and peeling from the effects of weather exposure. Two large, black garbage bags were leaning against the trailer next to the door. Both bags looked to have been torn open by some animal, probably another rabid dog, garbage was scattered around what passed for a front yard. Paper plates and wrappers had blown up against the hay bales positioned along the bottom of the trailer.

I knocked again, at no surprise, no one answered. I did notice a curtain twitching in the trailer just across from Rikki's. I knocked one more time before I tried the doorknob. The door was locked, but I turned the knob hard and continued to apply pressure and gradually felt the cheap inner working of the device giving way. Something suddenly snapped, and the door swung open.

"Hello, hello. Anyone home?" I called then waited for an answer. I felt inside for a light switch, found one, flicked it on and off with no result. I pulled the aluminum frame of the screen door open and stepped inside.

"Hello," I called again and waited for an answer. Between the moonlight beginning to filter in and the light from a streetlight down the lane, I could make my way through the place. Something scurried across a floor off to the side in the kitchen area. From what I could see, in the dim light the place was a mess.

I tossed her mail on the floor then moved down the hall toward the bedroom in the back. I flicked two light switches along the way with no result. It would appear the power to Rikki's trailer had definitely been turned off.

At the far end of the trailer, what served as a bedroom door stood open and hung at an odd angle. Upon closer inspection, the top hinge had been torn out of the cheap door. The double bed was unmade, and a couple of dresser drawers were pulled open. Various articles of clothing littered the floor and were mounded up along one side of the bed. The place didn't appear to have been ransacked as much as it looked like Rikki was just a total slob. The same cheap perfume smell I'd picked up from that hallway in the Lumberyard seemed to cling to everything in the bedroom.

I headed back down the hallway toward the front door. Something else scurried along the kitchen cabinet as I approached, and I stamped my foot for good measure, which set off another scurry before everything grew quiet.

I pulled the front door closed behind me and wandered over to the unit across the way where the curtains had been twitching. At least this unit had a functional screen door, not to mention a doorbell that worked and lights.

# Fourteen

A male voice called from inside. He sounded nervous, with maybe just a hint of having been caught in the act of doing something he wasn't supposed to be doing. "Just a moment, please. Who is it?"

"Hi, sorry to bother you, my name is Dev Haskell. I'm actually looking for your neighbor across the way, Rikki."

"Rikki? I haven't talked to her for a day or two."

"Would you mind opening the door? I'm having trouble hearing you."

"Ahhh, yeah, sure, just give me a minute. I'm moving a little slow these days, injured on the job," he said. I waited out on his wooden stairs for what seemed like five minutes before he finally opened the door.

He was tall and thin, with a shaved head, a hook nose, and he looked like he weighed about a hundred-and-twenty-pounds soaking wet. He moved slowly and seemed to wince with the effort of opening the door. He wore a large white plastic neck brace over T-shirt. The brace held his head in place and covered his shoulders like a pair of football shoulder pads. The whole affair was then strapped across his chest and extended down to the bottom of his ribs.

I immediately felt sorry for bothering the poor guy. "Look, I'm really sorry to bother you. I was just across the way looking for Rikki and saw your lights on."

Since he couldn't turn his head, he shifted his feet, so his entire body faced me, then he groaned and said, "Sorry, after the accident, I'm just not moving as fast as I should." He gave a half-hearted laugh then appeared to wince with the pain.

"You okay?" I asked.

"I'll make it, I think, I hope. I just want to get back to work as soon as possible. I'm sorry, who'd you say you were?"

"Names Haskell, Dev Haskell, I'm looking for your neighbor, Rikki."

"If you paid her in advance, she's probably already out spending it somewhere," he said.

"No, nothing like that. I just wanted to talk to her about another matter I think she might be able to help with."

"Talk to her?" He said like the idea of talking with Rikki had never really occurred to anyone before.

"Yeah, apparently she's out, at least she didn't answer the door when I knocked. You wouldn't happen to have any idea where she might be, would you?"

"You with the insurance folks?" he asked and winced with the pain of having to speak.

"Insurance? No, I just wanted to talk to Rikki, see if she could help me find someone I'm trying to locate."

"So you ain't with them insurance folks?" he said, exhaling and seeming to relax a little more.

"No, I just—"

"Oh hell, come on in. Hale's the name, Marion Hale," he said, then stepped aside, and held the door open so I could come in.

"Actually, I'm looking for Rikki and I—"

"I could maybe help you with that. She's quite the busy lady. Come on, get in here, I ain't gonna bite."

I stepped in, and Marion closed the door behind me. "You sure you ain't one of them insurance folks?"

"No, I'm not with any insurance company."

"Cause I ask you, you gotta tell me, can't be lying to me, or it ain't gonna stand up in court."

"Court? Honest, I'm not sure what you're talking about. I'm just looking for Rikki. Turns out she was actually with someone last night, and I've been trying to find the guy. I was hoping she could help."

"Bet she picked him up at the Lumberyard, right?" he asked, then started to unstrap his neck brace.

"Yeah, at least it would appear that's the case. I don't have a problem with Rikki. I just want to find the guy she was with. Say what's with the brace, should you be taking it off?"

"Sorry about that. I was afraid you was one of them insurance fellas. God, this damned thing is a pain in the ass, borrowed it from a pal. Can never be too careful, you know. I been on disability and got a worker's comp claim in the works. Of course the idiots denied it. Said I was out deer hunting and drinking up a storm. Don't know how they found out about all that, the bastards. Anyway, borrowed this here thing to make it look a little more real. Let me tell you, it ain't any fun having to strap this damned thing on and then pretend to limp around every time I go out."

"Yeah, I imagine that could get old pretty fast."

"You don't know the half of it," he said, pulling off the brace and tossing it in the corner. "How 'bout them beers?"

"Help yourself, but I better take a pass."

Marion gave me a strange look, then opened his re-frigerator. "Suit yourself. You don't mind me saying you kind of look like shit. I'm thinking like you could maybe use a little pick me up. Bad fall or something?" he asked, studying my face.

"Yeah, something like that. You mentioned you might be able to help me locate your neighbor, Rikki."

"Yeah, you wouldn't be the first poor bastard who showed up looking for her. Like I said, she's one you definitely never want to pay in advance. I think the woman means well, but it's a pretty sure bet she's got a screw or two loose up there."

"Actually, I'm looking for the guy she's with, or at least was with last night, hoping to find him. I don't have any beef with her."

"You ain't some irate husband, looking to cut some poor bastards love-stick off, are ya?"

"No, nothing like that. More of a gambling debt deal, and I just want to arrange some payment terms, is all."

He sipped and nodded then said, "Gambling debt, that could be Rikki, she likes to play. What's he look like?"

"What's he look like? Dark, curly hair, a bit of a fat guy, maybe about my height." I held my hand up to indicate the height.

"He driving some fancy SUV that's been beat to shit?"

"A black Infiniti QX with a crease in the passenger door and a crack down the front windshield, silver rims."

Marion took a healthy sip then nodded. "Seen him, at least the car, they were here last night, but not for more than just a couple of minutes. Heard her screeching and laughing when they pulled up. It was sometime after midnight, God she can be loud, woke me up, so I was looking out the bedroom window. She went inside, put some jeans on and then they were out of here."

"This guy have on a brown leather jacket?"

Marion seemed to think about that for a moment then drained his beer. "Sure I can't get you one?" he asked, opening the refrigerator.

I shook my head.

"No, now that you mention it, can't be too sure if he had a jacket or not, I mean, I was half asleep, but I'm pretty sure she had one. The guy, he never went inside, just stood next to them trash bags out there. I think he was probably taking a piss. She waltzes right back out the door, some sexy dress on and all happy like. Then the two of 'em climbed back in his piece of shit car and just drove off."

"You didn't happen to see two little girls, with them, did you? Little, maybe just this tall," I held my hand at about waist height. "One with blonde hair, the younger one's a redhead. Four and five years old."

"Kids? Around Rikki? You gotta be kidding. No, thank God, didn't see nothing like that. She ain't the sort of woman you'd want your kids around. Means well, but there's just always gonna be a problem. You know the type?"

Unfortunately, I did. "Any idea where they might be headed?"

"Yeah, outta this dump," he said, then laughed and took a long healthy sip. "If old Rikki had anything to do with it, you just might find the two of them up there to the Grey Wolf."

"The casino?"

"Yeah, up on the res. Anytime Rikki has a couple of bucks to rub together, she heads up that way to win big, although I've never, ever seen her come back a winner. If she's got some poor sugar daddy on a leash, that would be as good a place as any to check. You said gambling debt… that would be a bad combination teaming up with her. Sure as hell, she'll lose whatever your pal gives her.

Christ, they even know her up there. For all I know they might be giving her a discount, not that it really matters, they're bound to get it back all the same," he said and raised his eyebrows.

"The Grey Wolf."

"'About the only place I can think of where she'd go."

"Okay, I guess I'll give it a try, Marion. Hey, thanks for all your help, it's been a pleasure, appreciate the info. Good luck on that workman's comp claim," I said and reached for the door.

"You thinking of going up there, maybe I could just tag along. You know, help you locate her and all."

"Thanks, Marion, but I'm not going there right now. I'll check it out tomorrow sometime."

"You find Rikki, you let her know we talked. Tell her I ain't forgot I paid her forty bucks in advance, and she damned well needs to still make good on that. I'm gonna hold her to it."

"I'll be sure to tell her."

"See that you do, appreciate it. How 'bout one for the ditch?" He asked, pulling another beer out of his refrigerator.

# Fifteen

I fled the Kare Phree trailer park and headed north up to the Grey Wolf Casino. The last thing I needed right now was Marion Hale tagging along in his insurance fraud get up.

The Grey Wolf casino was located in the middle of a vast Minnesota forest on the Cut Lake Reservation. Other than state-sponsored pull tabs, most forms of gambling are still illegal in Minnesota, so the casino industry has sprung up on reservation lands, heralding a badly needed source of revenue and jobs. Sometimes it's been referred to as the second coming of the buffalo. It seems to have worked in a few cases, and the jury's still out on the others.

I could only hope Rikki and idiot Carlos were locked into a losing slot machine or suffering from eternal bad luck at the blackjack table. I put my foot down on the accelerator and pushed the car up to eighty miles an hour, tearing along the Minnesota back roads. I made it to Grey Wolf casino in record time and the better part of a tank of gas.

The casino wasn't just in the middle of a rural area. It was in the middle of about a thousand square miles of dark, dense forest. As I drew nearer I'd be going over a hill, and you could see the colored lights from the place reflecting in the night sky miles away.

It's more than a little strange to race along dark forest roads with the brights on hoping you won't hit a deer or moose and then suddenly come around the bend and you're suddenly face to face with this gigantic structure bathed in red, green, and yellow neon lights and all of them flashing and blinking.

Considering it was a weeknight, the parking lot was pretty full. I cruised through the parking lot twice, up and down the lanes looking for my stolen car, but I didn't see it anywhere. I did see a number of cars in the lot that were in much worse shape than the bomb I was driving. I estimated about every third vehicle parked in the lot was a pickup truck.

After cruising through the lot the second time, I decided to go inside and look for Carlos. Try as I may, the car was so long it hung out a few feet into the lane when I parked it. I couldn't pull ahead any further, so I just left it that way, hoped for the best, and hurried inside. The casino was like every other casino I'd ever been in. The moment you walk in the front door, you enter a completely different universe where you're assaulted by bells, whistles, and flashing lights.

I don't gamble. I learned a long time ago that everyone I've ever talked to who spent time in a casino will tell you they came home a winner. My experience has been I'm the guy they win the money from. I don't win.

I don't win on slot machines, I don't win at cards. You want to win at roulette, bet exactly the opposite of what I'm doing. I'm the worst when it comes to picking a winning horse or even dogs.

Nowadays, I can get in and out of Vegas and not spend five bucks on gambling. Besides, I'm usually spending my money buying expensive drinks for women who then either disappear or introduce me to their large, muscle-bound boyfriends that manage to show up at the end of the night.

Once inside, I started at the front door and worked my way along a curvy path toward the back of the football-field-sized, room looking for Rikki and Carlos. The carpet in the place was a royal green color with a pattern of hearts, spades, clubs, and diamonds. The place was hopping, and I kept searching little groupings of people. By the time I made it to the far end of the room, I felt like my eyes were spinning in opposite directions.

If I saw a woman with short, white-blonde hair that I thought might be Rikki, I stood nearby and called out her name, "Rikki." I must have done this at least a dozen different times and never got so much as a sideways glance. Of course, I'd only seen a black and white tape of Rikki, basically undressed, so I was working at a disadvantage.

There were a lot of fat guys strolling around the place, but none of them seemed to resemble Carlos. I didn't see any little girls, and I never saw anything even close to resembling a small pink suitcase.

I wandered back and forth past all manner of electronic machines ringing, beeping, buzzing, and flashing. I circled the blackjack tables, there were twelve. I circled the six dice games. I scanned the crowd around all three of the roulette wheels and peeked through the crowd at the two high stakes poker games. I came up empty-handed each and every time. I wandered aimlessly through the restaurants and even the ice cream bar, pretending to search for friends, but I never saw anyone who looked like Carlos and Rikki.

After two hours, I was beginning to think I'd driven up here on a wild goose chase, and I was busy silently cursing Marion Hale when I caught sight of the two of them. Actually, I didn't see them, at least not initially. I heard them first, along with everyone else in the immediate area, at no surprise they were in the midst of causing a scene.

Carlos and Rikki were sitting on a couch next to a fireplace. Carlos had his feet up on a coffee table, and Rikki seemed to be frantically trying to get the attention of a waitress. The staff was doing an excellent job of ignoring both of them.

The two of them were busy yelling back and forth at one another, and the couple who had just sat down opposite them a moment before in the hopes of enjoying the fire were already back on their feet in search of a more peaceful retreat. Everyone walking past stared for a brief moment, and then quickly picked up their pace.

"Listen, bitch. You can start throwing some gratitude my way any time now. It ain't been a picnic for me, let me tell ya."

"Gratitude? For what, you're lousy card playing? For grabbing my ass every damned time I turn around? Making me get my own drinks? Speaking of which, just where in the hell is someone who works here? I need another drink."

"What? Listen, little lady, I've been paying the freight since we got up here, and now I'm the bad guy for wanting some action in return? Feel free to pull your thumb out and start hitchhiking back to the Lumberyard anytime you want."

"Yeah, right, how 'bout we just agree you've been getting what you want a lot more times than I can count, which is way more than I can say for me, Mr. Short Hitter. You know what? I just need a damned drink, and then I just want to go back and sleep Carlos, and this time I want to be left alone. I mean it," she said, then shouted. "Hey, I could use another drink over here if anyone is listening."

"Will you keep it down, bitch? I already told you I don't want to draw anymore attention."

"Oh, yeah, right, how could I forget? You don't want to attract any attention because you play guitar with U2. Wasn't that what you told me? Give me a break, you big phony. You can't even whistle a tune for Christ's sake, let alone play guitar."

"Shut up, bitch."

"Oh yeah, and just what the hell are you gonna do about it? You gonna make me? Hey everybody, come on over here and see the rock star," she shouted to the crowd beginning to form at a safe distance around the two of them.

"I told you to shut up, bitch."

I was hoping Carlos would do something stupid like coldcock Rikki. I looked around for something to hit him with and focused on a wooden stool sitting in front of a slot machine. Unfortunately, just as I got to the stool, two rather large, muscle-bound individuals approached Carlos and Rikki.

One of the guys was wearing braids and had a nose that looked to have been broken more than once. Both the gentlemen were larger than Carlos, and both wore black T-shirts with the word "SECURITY" across their broad shoulders in large white letters. Even just standing there calmly and smiling politely, they appeared intimidating.

# Sixteen

They stood on either side of Carlos. Although they weren't touching him, they were standing close enough to him that he would have had difficulty getting to his feet without pushing one or both of them. The guy with the braids spoke in a tone soft enough that I couldn't hear what he was saying. As he spoke, he moved his hands up and down in a calming motion, from time to time, he nodded. He looked like he was explaining something obviously rational and appeared to be the very picture of a calm, reasoned response.

Carlos suddenly exploded and yelled, "But you're not listening to me. I just told you guys, this bitch was the one yelling and causing the scene, you should throw her ass out of here, not me. Hell, I'm your customer, I'm the guy picking up the tab for this ungrateful witch."

"I need another drink, damn it," Rikki screeched then tried to look beyond the gathered crowd for a waitress. Not seeing one, she slung her purse over her shoulder and started to leave. The security guy with the braids stepped in front of her and cut off her exit.

"Just what in the hell is your problem? Get the hell out of my way. I need another drink, and since the service in this joint is so shitty, I guess I'll just have to go and get it myself."

He said something to her I couldn't hear.

"You can try, pal, but I'm not going anywhere until I get me that drink. Now get the hell out of my way," she said and tried to push him. He didn't move, and Rikki had to take a step or two back to maintain her balance.

"See, exactly what I told you guys was happening. Believe me, I've had more than enough of her bitching, so go ahead and throw her ass out of here. Like I said before, she's the one who's been causing all the problems. It sure as hell ain't me."

The other security guy, the one without the braids, shook his head. He pulled a radio off his belt and began talking into it.

Rikki suddenly stepped in very close to him and whispered something into the guy's ear. Then she shrugged, giggled, and rubbed herself against his arm before whispering into his ear one more time.

He looked down at her, smiled, and shook his head no.

That got a reaction. "What in the hell is wrong with you? With both of you? You know what, you can just forget it. Now, I'm going to go get my drink, and there's nothing you can do to stop me," she said just as three more security guys showed up, all very large, and none of them smiling. Their arrival put a different spin on Rikki's last statement.

There was now a ring of security around them, and the guy with the braids seemed to explain a couple of things, looking from Carlos to Rikki. He was still speaking softly, but he wasn't smiling at this point. One got the immediate impression that he wasn't inviting much discussion, either.

"Oh, this is just great, happy now, bitch?" Carlos yelled as the security team began to move the two of them toward the front door. Carlos and Rikki had no choice but to go with the flow. I followed a discrete distance behind.

"You can't do this. What about my rights?" Rikki said and attempted to plant her feet and not move.

One of the guards effortlessly scooped her up like a big bulldozer and carried her along with the group.

"Don't you touch me," she screeched as they continued moving through the room. Heads turned and stared as the ensemble passed by.

About halfway across the main floor, the group took a hard right and headed for a door labeled "Hotel." They walked down a long hallway with framed prints of lake and forest scenes toward the hotel lobby. I hung back in the lobby until they made their way to the bank of elevators. Once everyone boarded the elevator, I hurried over and watched as the ascending floor numbers flash, counting off the floors above the elevator door. The flashing halted on the number six.

I waited a few minutes then pressed the button for the elevator, once it arrived I stepped on and pushed the button for six. I stepped back out on the sixth floor a moment later. The elevator doors opened up onto a wide hallway with grey pattern carpet and a contemporary looking table with a large pottery bowl sitting on it. For some reason, I touched the pottery bowl only to find it was somehow attached to the table.

The doors to all the guest rooms in the hall were in pairs, side by side, with a little porch light, mounted on the wall next to each door. The pinewood trim around each door was stained with a dark walnut stain. The doors themselves were metal and painted grey. An attachment was mounted just above the doorknob to insert your security card. Brass numbers just below the porch lights identified the room numbers. I took a couple of steps down the hall and saw the security guys heading back toward me and the elevators.

"What a pair of assholes," one of them said just before he saw me, and then they all grew quiet as we passed in the hallway. One of them giggled a couple of steps after they passed by.

I walked down the hall and around a corner. A room service tray with a plate of half-eaten pancakes and a full coffee cup sat on the hallway floor just outside a door. The tray looked like it had probably been sitting there since this morning.

Further down the hall, a security guy stood in front of a door with his arms folded. My guess was to make sure Carlos and Rikki remained in their room. He did not appear to be all that happy with his task.

As I drew closer, I noticed he had a tattoo of a war shield with eagle feathers hanging from it on one of his rather large biceps. He wore an earpiece in his right ear with a curly white cord running along his neck and down the back of his shirt. A thick ponytail of straight, dark black hair was pulled tightly behind his head and hung down his back. He had dark eyes, prominent cheekbones, and his nose looked like it was quite familiar with the boards around a hockey rink.

"How's it going?" I said as I walked past.

"Have a nice evening," he said, and nodded, but didn't crack a smile. I could hear Carlos and Rikki still arguing from behind the door to the room as I walked by. I made a mental note of their room number, six-thirty-one.

I rounded another corner in the hallway and cooled my heels for about ten minutes before I returned. The security guard was still stationed in the hallway, in the same position with his arms folded. He glanced at his watch, smiled, and nodded as I walked past. I couldn't hear any noise coming through the door behind him, so apparently Rikki and Carlos had quieted down.

I took up a position in a comfortable leather chair down in the lobby where I could watch the elevators. There seemed to be a constant flow of people either going to or coming from the casino.

About a half-hour later, the security guy with the ponytail came out of the elevator and ran across the lobby, obviously in a hurry. He had a hand pressed against his ear, holding the earpiece in place. He hustled across the lobby and back through the door labeled "Casino." I waited a few more minutes to make sure he didn't return before I took the elevator back up to the sixth floor.

# Seventeen

Once up on the sixth floor, I hurried down the hallway, past the breakfast tray with the pancakes, around the corner, and pressed my ear against the door labeled six-thirty-one. I couldn't hear anything. I knocked on the door then put my finger over the peephole.

A gravelly female voice called from inside the room a few moments later with a very unpleasant, "Yeah."

"Room service, drinks, and a chilled bottle of Grey Goose vodka, compliments of management."

"You're kidding. Well, it's about God damn time, I've been trying to get a…." Rikki opened the door and then stood there, staring at me for a long moment before she recovered. She looked around then said, "Wait a minute, you ain't got no vodka, what in the hell do you think you're doing. That security cop finally leave?" she said more to herself than me, then she leaned out the door glancing down toward either end of the hallway.

I shoved her back into the room then rushed past her, ready to attack Carlos. He wasn't in the unmade bed and he wasn't hiding on the floor alongside the bed. I glanced behind the curtains, then hurried past her and stepped into the bathroom. "Where's Carlos?"

"Who in the hell are you, and what in the hell do you think you're doing? You can't just barge into someone's room here. I know my damned rights, now you had better get your ass out of here before I call security," she said and struck a pose.

The room reeked of that same cheap perfume I first smelled at the Lumberyard, accented with a whiff of spilled liquor and the sharp tang of stale cigarette smoke just for an added effect. For the first time, I realized Rikki was wearing a red-sequined thong and a frown. She had what looked like hummingbirds in flight tattooed on either hip. A blue stone pierced her navel which was surrounded by tattooed flower petals. Deep ponds of mascara had pooled beneath her eyes and added a good twenty years to her face.

She seemed oblivious to her almost complete lack of clothing, and she struck a defiant pose by placing her hands on her hips and thrusting her chest out. Either that or she was showing off an estimated three grand worth of breast enhancement work. She stared at me without blinking.

"Where's that Carlos pal of yours?"

"That son of a bitch waltzed his fat ass out of here not more than ten minutes ago. Good riddance is all I can say. What a damned loser," she said and then strolled over to the table against the wall, pulled a cigarette out of an almost empty pack, and fired it up. She took a long drag, blew a cloud toward the ceiling, then crossed her arms and said, "Hey, what in the hell happened to you, anyway? Don't mind me saying, you really look like shit, man. What? You try this routine before and maybe got a little more than you could handle?" she said and chuckled.

I ignored that last line, walked over to the window, pulled the drapery back, and looked out into the crowded parking lot below, thinking I might be able to spot Carlos. A police squad was just pulling into the lot with its lights flashing and racing toward the main door of the Casino. I hoped they weren't going to come up here looking for Rikki.

"Is Carlos going to come back?"

"God, I sure as hell hope not. I've had just about enough of his asshole routine. You some kind of friend of his?" she said, then blew another giant cloud of blue smoke up toward the ceiling again.

"Where are the girls?"

"Girls? What girls? It's just me here, buster, and let me tell you something, pal, I was a hell of a lot more than your limp friend Carlos could handle," she said, then immediately changed her tone, raised her eyebrows, and smiled at me. "Interested?"

"Not really, at least not right now. What I am interested in is the two little girls he had with him. A blonde and a redhead, two little kids, four and five years old. Emma and Ava."

"Oh, yeah, them two. The cry babies. We left them with a girlfriend of mine.This joint ain't no place for kids. Besides, I don't want them cramping my style. You know?" she said and blew another cloud of smoke, seemingly satisfied with her maternal instincts.

"Left them with a girlfriend? She a friend of yours?"

"No, I don't even know her, that's why she's my girlfriend. Hello, yeah, she's a friend of mine. We dance together at the Lumberyard. Jesus, how do you think I know her?" she said and thrust her chin out indignantly.

"You better put some clothes on, we're going to go get them from her, now. For your sake, they better be okay."

"Now you just hold on here a minute. Just who in the hell do you think you are? I ain't ready to go and…."

"Let me explain something to you, Rikki. Those two little girls, the ones you left with your girlfriend, they were kidnapped by that close personal friend of yours, Carlos. Right now, you got the cops, and you got the feds looking all over for those kids as well as for your pal, Carlos. If you know where they are, you better take me to them now. If you don't, we'll just call the cops from here, you'll be an accessory to the kidnapping, you'll get charged, and I can guarantee you'll be found guilty and end up doing at least seven years."

"Wait just a damn minute, here. I didn't know anything about any of this shit. Honest, he didn't tell me them two was kidnapped."

"Did he show up with the girls in the car at the Lumberyard?"

"Well, yeah."

"It didn't strike you as strange some guy would leave two kids in the car, unattended, at night, and come in for a lap dance?"

"That don't prove nothing, and I didn't know anything 'bout them two until I got in his damned car, anyway."

"Were they crying? Did they maybe ask for their mother? Did they look frightened, scared? Hell, they probably asked you for help, begged you to do something, anything. But, I guess you decided it would just be more fun to dump then at someone's house and go off and party."

"Yeah, err, no, well, I mean not exactly. Hey, come on, they didn't tell me they were kidnapped or anything. Jesus, those two little brats, They were crying so hard I couldn't understand a word they was saying. Carlos told me they were upset 'cause they just wanted to go to the casino, and he wouldn't let them."

"Yeah, that's what they wanted, Rikki, at four and five years old of course they wanted to go to the casino with Carlos. I tell you what, lady, if anything should happen to either one of those little girls, you won't have to worry your little blonde head about serving any time."

"Why's that?"

"Because as sure as I'm standing here. I promise you, I'll come back and kill you, myself."

# Eighteen

er eyes grew big and round, and she sneered, "You, you can't just barge in here and talk to me like that."

"I just did, now get your ass dressed, you got one minute before I call the cops and you end up as an accessory to a kidnapping."

"But my hair, I mean, look at me, I'm a mess. You can't expect me to go out looking like this."

A little silvery, shiny, sequined thing hung in the closet area next to the bathroom. I pulled it off the hanger and tossed it to her. "Put that on, and hurry up, now you got less than sixty seconds before I call the cops."

"But…."

I pulled my cellphone out. "I'm so not kidding you, Rikki. I'll call the cops, and I couldn't care less if they lock your ass up for the rest of your worthless, life. Besides, I'm reasonably sure there are a number of other things they'd be very interested in discussing with you."

"Okay, okay, Jesus, would you ever just calm down? Maybe think about taking a chill pill or something, man," she said, slipping the slinky dress on over her head. She was attempting to wiggle into the thing, moving seductively from side to side with her arms extended up and over her head. "Hey, mister, come on, give a lady a hand, a little help here couldn't hurt," she said as the garment seemed to get hung up around her shoulders and piled up in front of her face.

I snugged the garment down over her two enhancements and along her side. The dress slinked down to maybe three inches below the fluttering hummingbirds on her hips and clung to her like a second skin. With the exception of a one-inch band that attached behind her neck, the dress was backless and featured a neckline that seemed to plunge down almost to the blue stone piercing her navel. It looked like she might bounce out of the top, and you could see her red-sequined thong flash when she moved her hips back and forth in an attempt to wiggle into the thing.

There was a price tag hanging from the band behind her neck and a large, white plastic disk resting against her lower back. The disk was a security tag, which strongly suggested that the dress had been stolen. The open back extended down and revealed a lacy tattoo on her lower back and the red elastic waist band of her thong.

"This thing is hot," I said.

"That's exactly why I got it, figured a guy like you might just appreciate all the options. So, now all of a sudden, baby's starting to think about all the fun he just might have right here at the end of his hot little fingertips," she said and leered up at me.

"Sorry to disappoint, but not really. What I meant was, you stole it, Rikki. The security tag is still attached to the back."

"Oh shit. That ain't good."

"Gee, you think? Too late to do anything about it now so come on, let's get out of here."

"Get out of here? What if this sets off an alarm at the front door or something? I'm liable to get arrested."

I reached up and yanked the price tag off. "Guess that's the chance you'll have to take. Maybe you should have thought about that before you stole the damned thing. Come on, grab your shoes, and let's go, now. I need to find those little girls. Let me just warn you one more time. You try and do something stupid, and the cops will lock you up and throw away the key. I'm not kidding here, Rikki."

"You're really just tons of fun, ain't you?" She said and picked up some sparkly silver heels from alongside the bed. "I think I'll just carry these til we get outside," she said and then yanked my bomber jacket off a plastic hanger near the door and draped it over her arm.

We took the elevator down to the lobby. Barefoot Rikki attracted all sorts of attention in her shimmering sleaze outfit as the sparkling red thong flashed against her thighs with every other step. Rather than cut through the casino, we exited out the front doors of the hotel lobby. Mercifully there wasn't a detector at the door that the security tag on her stolen outfit would set off. I'd taken hold of her by her wrist, and we were moving pretty fast toward the car.

"Oh, for Christ's sake, what's the rush? Can you just slow down and hold up for a bit? Give me a minute to slip into these heels, will you. God, this parking lot is tearing my damned feet to shreds."

"Make it fast. I want to get to those little girls."

"All right, all ready, all right. God, sorry I don't want my feet to bleed all over your car. Just calm down, a couple of seconds ain't gonna make that much difference one way or the other. Hey, exactly where in the hell did you park, anyway?"

We continued walking through the parking lot. I kept a lookout for my Infiniti just incase that fat scumbag Carlos suddenly appeared. Now there were a number of squad cars parked haphazardly in front of the main doors to the casino. Their red and blue roof lights were still flashing and seemed to be synchronized in time to the neon lights blinking off and on across the length of the casino.

"Oh, oh, looks like someone's going to be in trouble," Rikki slowed down and giggled. I yanked her wrist to pull her back in step.

A few minutes later, Rikki laughed and said, "Look at that piece of shit. Can you believe it? God, the things people drive. Who would ride in that thing, let alone drive it anywhere?"

"Thanks, Rikki, I hope you'll enjoy the adventure. That's what we're going to be riding in."

"You're joking?" She said, giving the car a thorough once over. Her eyes settled on the torn convertible top. "You gotta be kiddin? Is this thing even safe? Hell, is it even *legal*."

"Just get in, Rikki," I said. As I yanked the passenger door open, it gave off an ear-splitting creak. Rikki looked in at the long bench seat running from the passenger door over to the steering wheel.

"Charming, not. Jesus, look at the size of this damned thing," she said, then pulled on my bomber jacket and slid in. Once in, she caught sight of the mattress in the back and stared for a very long moment. As I climbed in behind the wheel, she reached over the seat and pulled up one of the hosiery restraints and tugged on it.

"Well, what do you know? Maybe we can have a little fun after all. What do you say? You a player?" she asked, then raised an eyebrow suggestively and ran her tongue across her upper lip. "Maybe just pull over to that dark corner at the far end of the parking lot, and we can get a little something going here."

"You just get me to those little girls, Rikki."

# Nineteen

We roared down the dark highway heading south toward the twin cities. I wasn't just speeding. I had the thing floored. I wanted to get the girls, rescue them, and end this nightmare. Carlos and even Tubby, for that matter be damned. Screw the money. They could deal with it and do whatever they wanted. They would anyway. I just wanted to get the girls back to poor Isabella.

I didn't think it was possible, but the top was flapping even louder than before and was now completely torn all the way across. With the wind whipping through the tear, I had the heater on, blowing full blast.

We were leaving a black cloud of sooty exhaust in our passing, and I was sure we were in violation of a number of pollution control laws. From time to time, Rikki would glance into the backseat to stare at the mattress and restraints then rub my shoulder or my arm. I continued to ignore her.

After the better part of an hour, she shouted over the roar of the torn top, "God, what's with the seats in this thing, something keeps poking me in the back."

"It's probably that security tag on the back of your dress."

"Oh yeah, I didn't think of that. So, like what's the deal, do these kids belong to you or something?"

"No, they're a friend's."

"Oh, so a girlfriend?" she said and raised an eyebrow, you could see the wheels beginning to turn in her head.

"No, not a girlfriend."

"You must be a pretty nice guy, then," she said and began to massage my shoulder and the back of my neck. As good as that felt, the last thing I needed was someone like Rikki in my life at any time, let alone right now.

"Actually, I'm not a very nice guy. In fact, women seem to run away from me all the time. They file restraining orders, tell me to never, ever, call them again, block my phone calls, spray paint mean things on the side of my car. I've had a couple of husbands after me, some women have moved completely out of the state to get away, a few threatened to have me killed. One or two have even tried."

"Oh, so you're a pretty bad boy, sounds like it could be kind of exciting," she said, then snuggled a little closer to me and ran a finger back and forth along my ear. "Who knows what's in store?"

"They all seem to get kind of tired of me after a while. Most of the time it doesn't seem to work out the best for either one of us."

She nodded like this made complete sense. "Is that what happened to your face? Looks like you took an awful pounding. Was it a crazy husband? Or, maybe jealous boyfriend, right? I mean, if you don't mind me saying, you really look like shit. If you know what I mean?"

"Yeah, I think you mentioned that before, it seems to be a pretty common sentiment. No, to answer your question, it wasn't some crazy husband. Actually, what happened was your sometime-pal Carlos blindsided me, then grabbed those little girls, along with a big chunk of change."

"Oh. My. God. You mean to tell me all that cash he had stuffed in that little pink suitcase, all that cash he was gambling with was yours?" She snuggled closer and started to run her hand up and down my thigh.

"He sure as hell didn't earn it. Let's just say none of that cash belongs to Carlos O'Kelly, and leave it at that."

"Carlos O'Kelly? You gotta be kidding me. You mean to tell me that's his last name, O'Kelly?"

"Yeah," I said, glancing over at her. Now it was my turn. "If you don't mind me asking, how in the hell could you not know his last name?" Then, I thought about some of the fast and furious, meet, and greet relationships that I'd had with women and figured it might be wise if I didn't comment any further.

She just shrugged and ignored my question. "Can I just ask you something?" she said then plowed ahead without waiting for my reply. "Just what in the hell do you do, exactly, that you carry that kind of cash around in a little pink suitcase?" She continued to rub her hand suggestively along my thigh.

"I wasn't carrying that cash around in the suitcase. That was your pal's gig. When Carlos took all that cash, he stuffed it in that suitcase."

"Sure, baby, whatever you say. I'm just thinking you must be pretty successful at whatever it is you do, and a girl can find that pretty attractive," she said and got a little more aggressive with my thigh.

I glanced at the speedometer and saw I was doing a little over ninety. I didn't need to be stopped for speeding in a car that didn't belong to me, spewing a black cloud of exhaust over the pristine wilderness with a woman wearing a stolen dress that I didn't really know. I let up on the gas and reached down and gently removed her hand from my thigh.

She frowned for half-a-moment before she said, "So, I was starting to work some magic, after all, wasn't I?" Then she snuggled in a little closer to me, rested her head on my shoulder, and gave a little sigh.

"I need to get to those little girls."

"Sure, baby, whatever you say, and we need to get that cash back, too. Then you should probably think about doing something to celebrate." Her smile suggested she suddenly knew way more than she had just a moment before.

"I need to get those little girls first."

"The thing I can't quite figure out is, if you got all that dough, why in the hell are you driving around in this piece of shit? I mean, with all the noise, it makes it kind of hard for a girl to whisper nasty little things in your ear. And what the hell happens when it rains? God, can you just picture me in the back with my arms and legs all bound up? Just think, I'd probably need a life jacket if you had me all tied up back there, and it rained," she said, then placed her hand back on my thigh and started massaging again.

"This isn't my car."

Rikki glanced over her shoulder into the backseat at the mattress and the restraints. She looked more than a little disappointed. "Well then, if it doesn't belong to you, where did you get it?"

"I sort of borrowed this from a guy."

"You sort of borrowed it? That sounds like you ripped the thing off, no offense, but I can't believe you'd actually choose this thing to steal. Of course, if that's the case, well then, where's your car?"

"My car? Well, that's another thing I plan to get back from your pal, Carlos, just as soon as we meet up."

"You mean to tell me that piece of shit he's driving around in is really your car? God, that almost makes this thing look like a step up."

"I don't know if that's exactly the way I would choose to describe it, but yeah, he took my car, and I want it back."

"So let me get this straight, you keep a suitcase full of cash, lots of cash and you own a car that ain't worth more than about ten bucks. You realize the thing is all dented up and the windshield's cracked. Was it like that before you let Carlos use it?"

"I didn't let him use it, he just took it, stole it actually and yeah, it had a series of incidents prior to becoming stolen property."

"God, I don't know. Hey, you got anything to drink in here? I think I could use a little something to keep me in the mood right about now."

"Sorry, but I'm fresh out."

She slid back over against the passenger door and seemed to be in deep thought for a few minutes. Occasionally, she would glance over her shoulder at the mattress and shake her head. She attempted to adjust the heater, but it was already on full blast. Seemingly bored, she opened the glove compartment and rummaged through a stack of papers crammed in there.

"Well, look at what I just found," she said and triumphantly held up a half-pint bottle that was slightly less than a third full. I couldn't read the label, and in the moonlight, the contents appeared to be less than appealing.

"What is it?"

"Who the hell cares?" she said, gave a shrug and then unscrewed the cap, put the bottle to her lips and took a big swig.

"Any good?"

"Oh, yuck. It tastes like someone might have pissed in the bottle or something," she shook her head and seemed to shutter.

"That might not be far from the truth."

She placed the bottle to her lips, took a couple more gulps, and seemed to think for a moment. "Yeah, definitely, God, that's bad," she said then rolled down the window and tossed the bottle out onto the road.

# Twenty

Rikki settled into the corner of the seat, stretching her legs out until they were up against mine and then proceeded to massage my thigh with her toes. After a while, she sat up and said, "Okay, Double X is the next county road, it will be on the righthand side, just after you cross some railroad tracks up ahead."

We went over a slight rise with some railroad tracks, the turnoff for Double X was immediately after that and I had to hit the brakes hard not to miss it. Rikki slid across the bench seat and back up against me as we skidded around the corner. She didn't move back to her corner once I straightened out, instead, she leaned into me and pressed even closer. The slinky, sparkly silver skirt had slid up to about where the hummingbirds were tattooed on her hips, and I had to use all my concentration to focus and keep the car on the road. We drove around a long gentle curve with what looked like open pasture on either side of the road.

"Dee just lives over in this development coming up, you want to take the first left," she said a minute or two later. All sorts of new homes suddenly seemed to spring up out of nowhere on the lefthand side of the road, occasionally, there was a light on in one of them. A moment later, a lane on the left came into view.

"Yeah, turn here and then just follow the street around for a few more blocks," she said.

The street wound round in a gradual curve. A series of short, dead-end streets with maybe ten town-homes on either side spun off the main artery as we curved through a neighborhood of duplicate structures. I lost count of the number of identical streets we passed before she said, "Take the next right, and Dee's place is the last house on the lefthand side."

I turned and drifted past a half dozen driveways, then slowed and parked in front of the last town-home on the left. The short street came to a dead-end about fifteen feet further on. I turned the ignition off then waited a good half-minute while the engine sputtered and coughed before it died altogether in one final explosion.

The town-home looked just like all the others on the street, two stories high with grey aluminum siding, white trim, a tuck under double garage and two gables on the roof.

All the shades were drawn, and the drapes on the ground floor were pulled closed. Other than the yellow porch light hanging over the front door, the place was dark. But then, so was every other home on the block at this early hour.

"Come on, honey, she's got an extra bedroom," Rikki said, then squeezed my thigh one more time before she slid across the seat to slip on those silver heels. I was out of the car and almost up the driveway to the front door before the passenger door creaked loud enough to wake the dead as she climbed out, and I automatically took a quick look around the neighboring units to see if any lights were flashing on.

She shuffled around the trunk of the car as I walked up to the front door, ready to ring the doorbell. There was a worn mat in front of the door that said, "Go Away."

"Hang on a minute, baby, I think her doorbell ain't working. Let me just give her a call," Rikki said, then pressed a speed dial button and waited. "Shit," she swore a moment later. "It went into her message center. God, I hope she didn't pick up some guy again and ended up at his place, no telling when in the hell she'll be back if that's the case."

I opened the screened door and pounded violently on the door for a very long moment. The noise echoed off the aluminum sided walls and seemed to bounce off the town-homes across the street.

About ten seconds later, Rikki waved at me, indicated her phone, and said, "Yeah, hi, Dee, glad we caught you. Are you home? Well, you better open up, honey, we're downstairs at your door." She made it sound like it was a special treat to have someone pounding on your door and making a social call in the middle of the night.

I pounded again.

"What?" Rikki said. "You're shitting me. He did? When? No, no, I didn't, really, I didn't. Well, I think you better open up anyway. See, the cops are kind of like involved, maybe. Hey, calm down, will you. Don't blame me. I didn't know, honey, honest. Okay, okay, just open the damned door, will you, Dee. We're standing out here in your damned driveway. My head is starting to kill me and I really, really have to use your bathroom, bad."

A moment later a light flashed on up on the second floor, that was followed by another one apparently illuminating the staircase and then finally one inside the entryway just on the other side of the front door. A hand pushed a curtain to the side, and a head suddenly appeared looking out the glass panel next to the door.

Then a woman I guessed was Dee opened the front door, looked at us, and said, "You are a royal pain in the ass, Rikki. What the hell do you want?"

"I'm sorry to bother you, I just want to get the girls, take them off your hands, and I'm out of your hair," I said.

Dee stood blocking the door in a ratty beige Terrycloth robe with brown trim. The Terrycloth belt was cinched tightly around her waist, and her arms were crossed in a no-nonsense pose. She did not look very happy. Her dark hair was matted on one side of her skull with a serious case of bed-head. She sported a fat lip and a black eye. She blinked awake as she registered the bruises on my face, then glanced past me at Rikki standing out in the driveway and just shook her head.

"You get that eye compliments of Rikki's friend, Carlos?" I asked, trying to build some rapport.

"Carlos? I'll shoot that bastard if I ever see him again. He came in here, all impressed with himself and then tried to grab some of my action without even paying. Now how in the hell am I supposed to dance looking like this, Rikki?" she yelled past me. "Huh, you tell me that, girl. Just what the hell am I supposed to do?"

Rikki had been hanging back about ten feet down the driveway, and she backed up another step or two when Dee shouted at her.

"Just what the hell am I supposed to do, bitch?" Dee yelled.

"Sorry to interrupt the discussion, ladies but I've come for those two little girls. I'll just take them off your hands, Dee, and let you get back to whatever you were doing," I said.

"What? She didn't tell you? I just told her a minute ago, that bad assed friend of her's, Carlos come and took both of 'em, right after he bitch slapped me around. Didn't pay me nothing, either. Rikki, you owe me fifty dollars, girl. I oughta just charge your ass a damned hundred dollars is what I should do. Coming over here unannounced with them two kids, bringing that Carlos into my life, and now this shit," Dee yelled past me again at Rikki, who backed a few more steps down the driveway.

"He came back here and took the girls? Did he say where he was headed with them?" I asked.

Dee focused her good eye on me. "Said he was going for a ride on his boat, planning to take a little vacation trip. You find him. You tell him he better just keep on going. I get hold of him there won't be enough of him left to wipe up off the damned floor. You hear that, Rikki? Your man Carlos is as good as dead if I ever have the misfortune to see his worthless ass again."

"Dee, honey, how was I supposed to know? Honest, I had no idea he was a frigging nut case," Rikki whined.

"You had no idea? That's about the only truthful thing you said in a long while. Truth is you never have any idea. You are completely clueless. You know what? From now on, I don't want nothing to do with the likes of you. You hear me, Rikki? Not one thing, I never, ever, want to see you again, ever. Just stay the hell away from me," she screamed.

"How long ago was he here?"

Dee gave a snarl as she looked at me. "Not more than an hour ago. God, I tell you, I barely got back to sleep once he finally left, and then you and Little Miss Easy Money started pounding on my door, phoning me, waking me up in the middle of the night and all."

"Yeah, I told Rikki not to do that. So an hour ago?"

"Well, it was probably more like about a half-hour. Them two little kids crying for their mama all night, I couldn't keep 'em quiet. I was thinking I should maybe call the cops, but then they finally fell asleep. Course, I ain't in bed more than ten minutes when Rikki's old love toy Carlos shows up. Then the two of you come storming in. And now this here is all the thanks I get," she said and turned her head to give me a better view of her fat lip and the black eye.

"A vacation trip and his boat. You got any idea where in the hell that might be?" I asked Rikki.

"He said something about having a boat over in Two Harbors. I figured it was just a pickup line and didn't think much about it, just thought he was feeding me a line and trying to impress me."

"Two Harbors?"

"Yeah, I guess. Who the hell wants to sit in a damned boat all night and freeze your ass off? I just figured it'd be a lot more fun to party over in the casino."

"Two Harbors," I repeated to myself and hurried down the driveway to the car. I reached for the car door and stopped then marched back to Rikki. Her smile seemed to grow with every step I took.

"I knew you couldn't wait, you know a good thing when you see it and believe me, I'm good, baby. So, you're looking for a little something before you get going. I got just the thing, and since we're friends, I'm gonna cut you a deal. How's two for one sound to you?" Rikki said, glancing over at Dee, then she smirked, cocked a hip, and flashed her sequins.

I reached up and yanked my jacket from her shoulders, then half spun her around and pulled the jacket off sending her forward a couple of steps toward Dee glaring in the doorway.

"Hey, what the hell do you think you're doing? Get your ass back here. You can't do that. I'm not done with you. Wait, a minute, I—I can give you a better deal. He can't do that, can he, Dee?" she screamed as I hurried to the car.

Rikki stood in the middle of the driveway with her hands on her hips and watched with a shocked look on her face as I climbed behind the wheel.

Just as she looked like she was about to say something else, Dee screamed, "You are such a stupid bitch." Then she slammed the door and turned off the front porch light. Rikki looked to be in shock as she stood there in the dark and stared at the closed front door. She turned back toward me with a look on her face suggesting she was about to open her mouth.

"Don't, just don't say a thing," I said.

"But what about me?" she said.

I reversed up the street and sped off.

# Twenty-one

The town of Two Harbors was over to the east and then north up Highway 61, running along the shore of Lake Superior. I shot across three counties doing about ninety miles per hour. I only stopped once to gas up, paid sixty-five bucks including two coffees, and kept going.

The forest on either side of the highway was a mixture of birch and pine. Then, once I hit Highway 61 along Lake Superior, the trees were interspersed with outcroppings and bluffs of red rock. I came around the bend and drove into the town of Two Harbors just as a hairline of grey signaling the dawning had begun to appear on the far eastern horizon.

The small municipal marina was the only place in town to dock pleasure boats, and so I headed toward it. The marina parking lot overlooked the harbor and had about twenty parking spaces. The lot was completely empty except for one other vehicle in the far corner, a black Infiniti QX with silver rims and some brand new damage along the driver's side.

Both of the doors on the driver's side were now dented and scraped with a residue of yellow paint extending from the front wheel, along the entire side of the car back to just behind the rear wheel. The rear bumper on the driver's side hung at an odd angle. I looked in the side window and saw a small doll lying on the backseat next to what appeared to be a Batman mask. I could only hope those little girls were okay and close. I hurried across the lot and then down a short set of stairs toward the white steel docks of the marina, trying not to make any noise.

I guessed there were maybe sixty slips for boats, and not all of them were filled. There didn't seem to be any activity at this hour coming from the boats that were tied up in the slips. I could hear my heart pounding as I quietly made my way along the docks checking for any semblance of life. The vast majority of the boats were draped in fitted canvas covers that were strapped and snapped onto the sides of the vessels as protection against the elements. I bypassed those covered boats and zeroed in on the handful that remained uncovered.

The first two boats I checked were empty and looked to have been that way for quite some time. On both of the boats, the entrances to their galleys were padlocked. As I approached the third uncovered boat, I could detect a bit of activity going on. It was a medium-sized Chris Craft cabin cruiser, blue and white with the name "Sick Leave" painted in gold letters across the rear.

It was definitely occupied. I watched as the boat seemed to gently rock from side to side.

Sounds were emanating from inside the vessel, but I couldn't make out what was being said. I heard some high-pitched squeals, and I thought if Carlos was in any way hurting those little girls, I wasn't going to be able to control my reaction. I cautiously peeked through the small, rectangular window on the side of the boat and into the small galley. I spied what looked like a couple of college kids locked in a fairly vibrant early morning embrace.

It was a toss-up which one was making more noise. I guessed the boat probably belonged to one of their parents, and much as I would have enjoyed rapping on the window to interrupt, I moved on.

In short order, I had checked out all the boats in the small marina and hadn't found the girls or Carlos. I started to panic, thinking they may have already left, and then it would be anyone's guess where they were headed. They could go south down toward Duluth with any one of a number of stops along the way, or worse head north up into Canada or even motor over into Lake Michigan in which case all bets were off. I stood looking across the harbor, out into the giant inland sea of Lake Superior and beyond at a complete loss of what to do.

Something clanked across the small harbor, metal against metal. I automatically glanced over, and that's when I saw him, Carlos. It looked like he was in the process of gassing up a fairly large cabin cruiser. He had two large grocery bags, brown paper with handles that he picked up, and then carried down into a galley. I moved as quietly as possible off the marina dock then began to do some serious running up the steps into the parking lot.

It was a flip of the coin if I'd get there faster running or taking the time to fire up the car and drive over. I figured if I ran, there'd be less of a chance Carlos might spot me, so I cut across the parking lot and began to round the dirt road along the edge of the small harbor.

By now, the slit of grey on the eastern horizon had begun to turn pink. Fortunately, there was still a little bit of early morning cloud cover keeping things in the harbor area a hazy grey. I picked up speed as I ran and prayed Carlos would stay below in the galley for just a few more minutes.

He had docked his cabin cruiser alongside a concrete pier next to a fuel pump. A hose was running from the pump into the fuel tank on the cabin cruiser. The pier had a series of car tires lashed along the side to protect boats from scraping against it when they pulled alongside. Sitting in the middle of the pier was a squat wooden structure with weathered clapboard siding and a cedar shake roof that apparently served as a store. Most likely it sold overpriced incidentals along with minnows and, of course, fuel. Windows were on all four sides of the place, and lights were on inside.

I was maybe thirty yards away and closing when Carlos climbed up from the galley then strolled along the lower deck, holding what looked like a glass of orange juice. He stood there sipping as he gazed out toward the lake with his back to me. As he sipped, his head seemed to slowly follow along the shoreline, gradually turning and studying the small marina where the two college kids were probably still going at one another. Then he turned around toward shore and ran his eyes along the road until he caught sight of me. He stood sipping and watching me for a very long moment.

He took another casual sip from his glass and watched as I continued running toward the pier and his cabin cruiser. It seemed to take a while before he registered on me churning down the road, he watched me for another long moment, and then something suddenly seemed to click, and he sprang into action.

He hurried up a little three-step ladder onto the upper deck, being careful as he climbed up not to spill his orange juice. He hurriedly glanced over his shoulder back in my direction just as I came up to the concrete pier. He turned the key in the console and pressed the starter button in an attempt to get his engine going, frantically glancing back a couple of times.

I could hear the starter grinding away as I gained on him. He threw another anxious glance over his shoulder and seemed to push the starter all the more as it continued to grind. He pounded the console with his free hand in a frantic effort to encourage the engines.

I ran up the concrete ramp leading onto the pier just as a grizzled looking guy with a cane came limping out of the wooden structure. He was dressed in overalls, with the sleeves rolled up on a red and black plaid flannel shirt. He wore a sweat-stained baseball cap at an angle and scuffed up work boots.

"Hey, hey," he yelled at Carlos. "Just what in the hell do you think you're doing, you idiot? Hey, God damn it, I'm talking to you. You hear me? You ain't paid yet. Stop it. You can't be going nowhere until you pay, damn it." He started taking some steps toward Carlos, all the while shaking his cane and continuing to scream incoherently as I shot passed him.

The engine suddenly caught and roared to life. Carlos glanced over his shoulder as I shot down the pier almost alongside him. He shoved the throttle down, and the boat lurched forward then halted for just a second as the two ropes lashed to the pier briefly stretched taut, and held.

I jumped and went sailing through the air as both steel cleats suddenly tore off from the fiberglass hull, and the boat shot forward. I landed on the rear corner of the lower deck then got banged across the back of my head as the hose that had been refilling the tank flew up into the air and flopped around on the concrete pier. I slipped backward, grabbing frantically along the slick fiberglass for a handhold. I clung onto a chrome corner railing, more decorative trim than anything else just as I was about to go over the side and pulled myself back into the boat.

Carlos continued to pick up speed as he rocketed past the sign declaring a "No Wake Zone," cleared the harbor and headed for open water. He glanced over his shoulder again, grinning this time after having made his escape. The sight of me suddenly climbing up the little three-step ladder and heading toward him on the second deck quickly wiped the smile from his face.

He cranked the wheel hard, first to the right and then to the left just as I stepped onto the upper deck. The boat lurching to one side, and then the other caused me to stumble and fall, more or less landing right at his feet. It was all the time he needed, and when I glanced up again, I was staring into the barrel of a pistol that looked an awful lot like the Sig Sauer I had stashed in my glove compartment, only from this angle the end of the barrel looked about the size of one of the tunnels I'd driven through racing up here on Highway 61.

"Looks like you're just gonna have to learn the hard way, once again," he said then smiled.

"You can keep the money, Carlos, I really don't care about it. I just want to bring those little girls back to their mother. Just pull back into the harbor so we can get off. I won't call the cops on you, I promise."

"Sure thing, no problem, I believe you," he said then laughed. "Just kidding, actually I'm pretty sure you'll probably just haul ass to the cops and then, in like thirty minutes, I'll probably have some helicopter hovering over me and once again, I'll get royally screwed. So, no thanks."

"Just let me take the girls and get them out of your hair. They're just going to slow you down, anyway."

"Oh yeah, right. Gee, now why didn't I think of that? No way, pal, those two little brats are the best insurance policy I got right now. So you're not going to be taking them anywhere."

"You don't think that guy with the cane back at the harbor hasn't already called the cops. You ask me, he looked pretty pissed off. After all, you took off without paying, Carlos. Hell, he probably thinks you stole this boat, too. Just in case he had any doubts, the moment he saw me jump on board at the last minute most likely convinced him something ain't right. Come on, man, the cops are probably firing up the SWAT team chopper right now. You stole enough cash to go somewhere, hell anywhere, but you're not going to make it with those two little kids slowing you down. Let me take 'em off your hands, and then you can really make tracks."

"No chance," he said, then cast his eyes to the sky and looked left and right. He seemed to think for a moment then said, "You know, now that I think about it, you just might be making some sense. I tell you what. I think it would be a good idea if you helped me."

"I can do that, let me—"

"Shut the hell up. For the time being, I want you to crawl over here," he said and then opened what looked like a cabinet door exposing some steep little steps leading into a galley area.

"So here is what we're gonna do, I need you to just lay your ass down on those steps going into the galley. No, not like that, turn around and roll over on your stomach, I want you head first, douche bag. You just point your head down into the galley, and keep those legs of yours up here on the deck."

"I'm telling you, you're wasting precious time, Carlos. Let me just take the kids, and you can make tracks, man."

"Will you just shut up and do it, I want any advice from you, I'll ask for it. Now come on, move, damn it," he said and gestured with the pistol giving me just about all the incentive I would ever need.

"Don't do this, man."

"Just move before I change my mind and give you another beauty treatment, only this time I'll use a baseball bat and then throw you over the side. By the way, anyone tell you, you're looking like shit?"

"No, I haven't heard that from anyone."

"Yeah, right. Come on, get your damned head down those steps before I forget about being such a nice guy," he said and then waved the Sig Sauer at the tip of my nose as an added incentive.

# Twenty-two

With my head hanging down the steps and into the galley, it was impossible to tell whether we were heading north or south. A number of small windows were along either side of the galley, but the curtains over them were pulled closed, and I couldn't see out. Occasionally, I raised my head and held it up for thirty seconds or so just so it wouldn't explode.

The galley consisted of a triangular-shaped table along one side with a carton of orange juice and a vodka bottle sitting in the middle of the table. A small cooking area and a little built-in refrigerator were just across from the table. There was a narrow countertop next to the two-burner range that was littered with a number of wrappers from McDonald's and what looked like leftover French fries.

From where I was positioned, basically upside down on the ladder, there was a door that stood directly opposite me at the far end of the galley. I guessed it was probably some sort of sleeping quarters, and with any luck, that was where Carlos was keeping Emma and Ava. A digital clock on a shelf above the counter with all the McDonald's wrappers displayed the time, just in case I needed to know exactly how many minutes I'd been forced to remain upside down.

Sometime later, I heard a distant noise that quickly morphed into the unmistakable sound of a helicopter passing overhead. I planted my hands on one of the steep steps into the galley and braced myself, so I could look up and over my shoulder as the helicopter slowly drifted into view. It seemed to hover off to the side while they apparently checked us out.

Carlos had thrown a beach towel over my legs as soon as the helicopter came into view. A figure dressed in bright orange and wearing a white helmet leaned out the open side of the helicopter and glanced down at us. After some time, he gave a wave as the helicopter drifted overhead and then circled us a couple of times.

Carlos gave an enthusiastic wave up to the helicopter, then flashed a broad smile as he groaned, "You bastards," under his breath. A moment later, the guy waved again, and the helicopter took off and headed further up the shore. I listened as the sound gradually faded into the distance.

"Well, there you go, how's that make you feel? So much for your good friends, the authorities doing anything to try and find you. I'd guess they just took one look at your sorry ass and came to the conclusion you simply weren't worth the effort," he said and chuckled at his own joke.

"Carlos, they're going to be looking at each and every boat they come across as they head to that little marina up in Two Harbors. Once they get there, they'll talk to that guy at the store. They're bound to spot my SUV, and they'll run the license plate. Then you'll have about ninety seconds to say your prayers. The only difference is next time they swing by, you ain't getting off with just a wave and a smile."

He seemed to think about that for a moment or two and said, "We'll just see about that." Then he took another hearty sip from his glass and let out a little satisfied gasp. Ten minutes later, he gave the wheel a hard turn to the right, and we were headed toward shore.

"Change your mind all of a sudden? I'm guessing that helicopter is heading back out of that Marina by now, and believe me, now they'll know exactly who in the hell to look for."

"I think it would be a good idea if you just stay put down there and shut up, smart ass," Carlos said, then he leaned over and gave me an ineffective kick that glanced off my side.

A few minutes later, I was aware of us riding a series of waves, rocking up and down, and then the next time I looked back over my shoulder, I could see the tops of birch trees.

"Not to worry, Haskell, by the time that helicopter comes back this way, it's gonna fly right past us," Carlos laughed. "Then, they'll probably head over to the Wisconsin side, on another wild goose chase. See how far they get with that. We'll be long gone, and they can just sit around with their thumbs up their asses wondering where in the hell we disappeared to."

We motored on for maybe ten more minutes, only now we were literally puttering at a much slower speed along a course that seemed to veer back and forth, left and right. In short order, the canopy of birch trees with their yellow, fall leaves grew substantially thicker, and I could hear birds chirping. After a bit we seemed to coast to a stop. Carlos slipped the engine into neutral and then just stood there looking like he was studying something.

"All right, you just hold real still now, dumb shit, and don't do anything stupid." He held the pistol along his side, but it was still pointed at me as he opened a drawer next to the entrance to the galley. "Yeah, perfect, this should do the trick. Just don't go getting any ideas about being some kind of hero," he said and pulled what looked like a roll of duct tape out from the drawer.

He straddled me, placing a foot on either side, then he pressed the barrel of the pistol against my spine and held it there for a long moment. "Just so we understand one another," he said.

He reached down suddenly and quickly wrapped the tape snugly around my ankles a number of times. Once my ankles were secure, he tore off the end of the tape. He grabbed onto my jeans with both hands and then dragged me back across the deck, pulling me up the gal-ley stairs until I was lying on my stomach. It felt good to suddenly be stretched out on a flat surface, and I took a number of deep breaths as the pressure gradually began to fade from my chest.

"Now, I want you to place both your hands behind your back. Come on, hurry up, I don't have all day," he said and poked me hard in the butt with the pistol then grabbed one of my wrists.

I put the other hand behind my back, and he quickly wrapped the tape around my wrists and forearms. He tore off a short piece of tape, rolled me over and placed the tape over my mouth then smoothed it down with his hands. He pulled me up by the shoulders, groaning with the effort as he moved me into a sitting position. Then he stepped behind me and dragged me over against the chair bolted to the deck in front of the console.

He was whistling now, enjoying the task as he tore off a long piece of tape. He wrapped one end around my forehead and the other end around the back of the chair so that my head was held firmly against the chair. Then, he wound the tape two more times around my head and the back of the chair until I was taped up against the thing and unable to move.

"I guess that should hold you. All wrapped up nice and tight for Christmas," he said as he stood and laughed, sounding half crazy as he did so. He reached over and drained what little was left in his glass, then he put the engine in gear and slowly moved forward. I could sense us making a complete circle, and then he guided the boat back and forth a few times, working the throttle and the wheel. A few moments later, I felt a bump as we gently brushed against something. Carlos turned the engine off and grabbed his empty glass.

"Well, I suppose its time to go meet the neighbors. I'm sorry you can't join me, but you seem to be rather inappropriately attired. I think it might be best if you just wait here for me. Not to worry, I won't be long," he laughed, then shoved the pistol in the back of his belt and pulled his shirt out to hide it. He gave me one last look and a little finger wave before he carried his empty glass down the ladder to the lower deck and then disappeared from view.

I could hear his footsteps as he walked along the side of the boat toward the front. He was whistling some nondescript tune for a moment, and then there were a couple of quick, soft footsteps, and I guessed he had probably jumped off onto a dock and tied the boat up.

I immediately started to try and wiggle my hands out of the duct tape. Not that it did much good. It seemed the harder I tried the more the length wrapped around my head felt like it was growing even tighter.

Carlos's voice interrupted my efforts when I heard him calling in the distance, "Hello, hello there. Hi, I hope you don't mind the interruption. I wonder if you might be able to help, I just tied up at your dock."

I lay still for a long moment hoping to make out more of the conversation, but all I could hear were birds chirping overhead in the birch trees. I attempted to try and pull one of my hands loose and then tried to simply rip the tape around my wrist, but nothing seemed to work.

After a while, I heard what sounded like faint pounding coming from the galley below. Someone was pounding on the door on the far side of the galley. A moment later, I could make out the sound of a soft, little voice. I figured it had to be either Emma or Ava. At least I knew they were on the boat, not that I was able to do anything about it just now.

Suddenly I heard the dull report of a pistol, two shots, and then maybe a half minute later a third. The shots echoed off the sheer red granite cliffs from somewhere nearby. The birds overhead in the trees stopped chirping, some crows called out and flew overhead and then everything remained deathly quiet.

Sometime later, I heard footsteps on the dock and then off-key whistling. Carlos suddenly appeared on the small ladder a moment later with a freshly filled drink and an idiotic grin on his face.

"Oh, shit, it looks like you're still alive. Oh well. Hey, guess what? The nice folks who live here said it would be okay if we borrowed their car," he said, then held up a set of car keys and dangled them in front of me.

"I guess you should just stay put. I'm going to get a couple of things organized and then we'll leave, just one big happy family. That sound okay to you? Hey, speak up, what's wrong man, cat got your tongue?"

I looked up at him as he flashed an idiotic grin.

"Well, okay, suit yourself, any way you just take it easy and stay put, this should only take a minute," he said. With that, he gave me another ineffective kick in the side. I acted like it hurt, but only so he wouldn't try the same thing again and maybe next time get lucky.

# Twenty-three

Carlos whistled away down in the galley, still off-key, and to be honest, I wasn't even sure if it was actually a tune. With my head taped to the console chair, I could barely get a partial view of what he was doing. He pulled a cushion off one of the benches beneath the galley table and tossed it on the floor. Then he lifted up the bench seat, reached in, and pulled out a bright pink suitcase. He smiled, set the suitcase on the table and patted it lovingly. He stepped to the far end of the galley, glanced around, and very cautiously pushed the door open.

"Okay, girls, its time to come out, you two, come on, it's okay. That's right, come on out here and see the surprise. You can see who came to visit us this morning. You'll never guess who it is."

Ava and Emma stumbled out from behind the galley door. They seemed to be all right physically, although they looked disheveled and still wore their little flannel nighties. They were most likely confused and frightened. At least they didn't look like they'd been beaten or hurt in any physical way. Both their faces were tear stained, and little Ava hung tightly onto older sister Emma's hand.

"We want our mommy," Emma demanded.

"Well, I guess she's still too busy to come for you right now, but come on, I've got a surprise for you. Look who's here instead, our old friend, see," Carlos said, then pulled the girls up toward the steps leading out of the galley. The two of them looked up and focused on me, not quite sure what to make of the figure wrapped up in duct tape and attached to the console chair.

"It's your pal, Dev. Remember? He was the man who gave you to me," Carlos laughed.

Emma jumped up the steps and Ava followed, they both landed in my lap with a thud and then wrapped their arms around me and hugged tightly.

Ava attempted to snuggle in even closer while Emma pulled back and stared at my face for a long moment. She wrinkled her nose and said, "You maybe don't look so good Dev."

I tried to nod in agreement, but couldn't move my head with all the duct tape wrapped around it.

Carlos threw the pink suitcase out through the little doorway past the girls, then he climbed up the steps and rattled what was left of the ice cubes in his drink. "Okay, here's what we are going to do. The nice people who live here are going to let us borrow their car, so I can drive you girls back to see your mom."

"Our mom," Emma screamed.

"I want my mommy," Ava said then started to cry as she snuggled deeper against my chest.

I strained at the duct tape around my wrists until my arms ached, but absolutely nothing happened, the tape remained in place.

"I'm going to load my suitcase in the car along with you two girls, and then if everyone is good, no crying and no saying bossy things, then I'll come back and get your friend, Dev. I think it would be a really good idea to take him with us, don't you?" Carlos said.

"Yes, he has to come with us. But, I don't think he can talk with all that tape covering his mouth," Emma said.

"I just had to put that over his mouth because he said some very bad words, and he needed to have a time out."

"Maybe he'll be good now," Emma said.

"I'm not so sure," Carlos said.

"I want my mommy," Ava cried.

"That's a very good idea, honey. Come on, let's all get in the car so we can go and see your mommy. There are a few things I'd like to tell her," Carlos said, then he picked up the pink suitcase, stuffed it under his arm, and ushered the little girls over to the ladder and down to the lower deck.

Once down, I could hear him helping the girls off the boat, telling them to be careful jumping onto the dock. I heard them land softly on the dock, and then he was asking them what their mom was going to make for dinner as his voice faded away.

# Twenty-four

Sometime later, I heard footsteps on the dock, heavier steps than the girls, and more horrible whistling. Carlos's fat head with that idiotic grin plastered across his face appeared a few moments later coming up the small ladder. He was holding a fresh drink, and he took a large sip and examined me over the rim of the glass.

"Well, just one more thing to load up, and then we'll be on our way. You bag of shit," he laughed and then kicked the soles of my feet just in case I wasn't paying attention.

"What's that scowl for? Oh, come on, don't be like that. I thought you'd want to go see mommy, too." he said and laughed. Then he bent down and pulled the end of the tape wrapped around my head. He unwound it from my forehead, around the back of the chair off my forehead, around the chair once more than he stopped.

"I should probably let you know this is liable to hurt quite a bit coming off your skin this time around. Oh well, one can only hope," he shrugged. "Who knows? It's liable to be an improvement. Go fast or slow, fast or slow. I just can't make up my mind. I suppose we'll just have to see."

With that, he yanked the final length of tape, hard. It pulled the hair from my scalp along the side of my head, then ripped about three layers of skin off my left temple, made a bloody path across my battered forehead, and then ripped the hair out from the other side of my head.

I tried to shriek, but my scream remained muffled behind the duct tape over my mouth.

"Oh come on, now, admit it. That was kind of fun, wasn't it? I mean at least I enjoyed it."

I was snorting in an attempt to get my breathing back under control, gradually slowing down the air intake.

"Oh, you strong, silent types. Well, okay, have it your way, come on, we've got places to go and people to see," Carlos said, then took a fistful of my shirt in either hand and urged me to my feet. I stood for a brief moment as he smiled just before he pushed me forward. With my ankles bound and my hands taped behind my back I fell face first, bouncing onto the wooden deck, banging the side of my head against the deck when I landed. I had to snort some more to get air back in my lungs, and I could feel the inside of my cheek swelling where I bit it when my chin hit the deck.

"Hmm-mmm, bit of a dilemma, I see. I don't suppose you'd care to hop down the steps, would you?"

I rolled over and shook my head no. I was afraid Carlos was going to throw me overboard all taped up.

"I guess I could unwrap your ankles, but I feel it's only fair to warn you. If you try anything stupid, well, I guess I'll just have to shoot you. Do I make myself clear? Do we understand one another?"

I nodded vigorously.

"Okay," he said, suddenly sounding very happy. Then he bent down and unwrapped the duct tape from around my ankles. When he was finished, he stood up and stepped back.

"I think you can get up on your own now," he said, then struck a pose with a finger raised over his head as if he were making a point in a speech. "Besides, you'll never learn if you don't attempt, if you don't at least try. Come on, I know you can do it," he laughed.

I half rolled onto my knees then glanced up at him, not knowing what might happen next.

"Come on. You can do it, you're halfway there, come on."

I leaned forward and got my right leg up, so I was in a genuflecting position.

"That's it, come on, I know you can."

I rose slightly and got the left leg up. Then, just as I began to stand, Carlos took a half step toward me and swung his leg up like he was kicking the perfect field goal. He caught me squarely on the chin and sent me back a few feet before I landed on my back. The fall knocked the wind out of me and bounced my head off the deck with an audible thunk, so hard that I saw stars.

"Wow, I bet that would have scored the extra point and won the game," he said, then took a healthy sip from his glass. "That was just to be sure we understand one another," he said, then walked over to the small ladder and stepped down to the lower deck.

"So, get a move on, for Christ's sake, you're wasting precious time, keeping the girls waiting and well, in general, just pissing me off. Stand the hell up and get your ass down here."

I took a couple of deep breaths in an effort to clear my head and fill my lungs. Things were still spinning inside my head, and I tried to blink my vision back to where it should be.

"I'm still down here waiting for you. Trying to remain patient while you continue to waste our precious time," Carlos called from below, sounding just a little bit more pissed off.

I struggled to my knees, then got my feet under me and slowly began to stand. I was still a little dizzy with things spinning, and I shook my head slightly to clear it then gingerly took a couple of tentative steps toward the ladder. My stomach threatened to erupt, and I had to hold very still for a moment before I stepped forward.

"About damned time," Carlos said, looking up at me.

I debated kicking him in the teeth, but the odds weren't that good that I'd be successful, and even if I was, then what? If he didn't die, he'd throw me in the water and watch me drown. Or, he'd shoot me and just watch me bleed to death.

"Tell you what, just turn around and I'll guide you down," he said then as I turned and lowered my right foot he gently held onto my ankle and guided my foot to the first rung. "Okay, now we're going to lower the left ankle down to the same level, so just bring it down, that's right nice and slow. Okay, same thing, right one first, good, good," he said, guiding my ankle.

I planted my right ankle on the second rung then moved my left ankle down toward the same level.

"Oh, Jesus, you know what? Screw this and just get your ass down here," Carlos yelled, he suddenly reached up, grabbed my belt, and pulled me off the ladder half throwing, half pushing me onto the lower deck.

I banged my head off the side of the boat on the way down then bounced off the chrome railing running along the back of the boat before I crashed onto the floor of the lower deck and then just laid there, doing a mental examination of which part of me hurt the most.

"God, you can sure make things difficult," Carlos said. He stood over me and took a long sip from his drink.

I lay on the deck, thinking I may have cracked a rib or two. My shoulder was killing me. I was definitely seeing double, and the stars were still flashing and spinning in my head.

"What the hell is it with you? I've never seen any-one so clumsy. Come on, get up, will you. This is taking forever."

I struggled to my knees, but just as I was about to try and get to my feet, Carlos kicked me in the rear, hard and sent me forward a couple of feet. I landed on the deck then tried to get up again, and he did the same thing. This time I just stayed down and waited.

Carlos took a couple of steps forward, then stood on my leg and began to slowly walk on me, when he got to the middle of my back he paused then started moving his feet back and forth, essentially wiping them on my shirt."

"You know, I can't be sure, but I think I might have just stepped in some dog shit out there in that yard. I wouldn't want to get the inside of that nice car dirty. I'd just feel awful if I did that. One just can never be too careful," he said and continued to wipe his feet on my back a few more times before he finally stepped off and dropped to the dock.

I remained stretched out on the deck trying to stop my head from spinning around, I felt like I might get sick, and I breathed in deeply in an effort to keep my stomach down. My efforts seemed to slowly be working.

"Still waiting," Carlos called from the dock.

There were more than a few things I wanted to say and do to him at this point. But they would have to wait. I groaned to my feet and slid up along the side of the galley as I attempted to stand. The chrome railing I had bounced off of before landing on the deck a few minutes ago was bent, twisted, and hanging loose from where it attached to the far corner of the boat. I moved to the side of the cabin cruiser and sized up the wooden dock where Carlos stood waiting alongside the boat, it was just about a one-foot drop, and for half a minute I thought about leaping on top of Carlos.

"There you are, finally. I was beginning to wonder," he said. He stood on the dock, wearing a disgusted look with his arms folded across his chest, looking for all the world like a disappointed parent about to deliver another lecture. Instead of the lecture, he took another long sip from his drink.

I stepped up to the edge of the cabin cruiser and jumped the foot down to the wooden dock, landing on my feet. After a half step or two, I regained my balance and cast a wary eye on Carlos.

"'About damned time, come on," he said, then followed up with another long sip before he turned on his heel and walked off the dock across what looked like a well-tended lawn toward a fairly fancy home.

# Twenty-five

The home was two and a half stories of split logs, and cedar shakes with dark green trim around the windows and along the peaked roof. A large granite patio spread out like a giant pond from the back of the structure. A massive fire pit at the far end of the patio was surrounded by comfortable looking padded chairs. A glass-topped table with a large umbrella and a dozen more chairs were arranged closer to the house. Two plates of what looked like half-finished breakfasts, a couple of coffee mugs and a coffee pot sat on the table. Two cloth napkins lay discarded and crumpled on the patio stone. Soft classical music drifted across the patio from speakers hidden somewhere.

A rushing stream was close enough to hear, although I couldn't see exactly where it was, and large bushes with red roses served as a hedge that bordered the back of the patio. Four massive log steps, about ten feet long, led up to a back porch that ran the entire length of the structure. A pair of double doors were set squarely in the middle of the log structure and looked like they led into a large kitchen. Three tall windows with flower boxes full of red and pink impatiens were on either side of the double doors.

Beyond the house and close to the fire pit stood a split rail fence bordering a gravel parking area that appeared to be home to a very nice black Mercedes. The car looked sleek, shiny, and very new. I could see the tops of two small heads bobbing around in the rear seat.

As we walked across the patio toward the Mercedes, I glanced at one of the large windows in the house and saw an older man and woman sitting back to back on two wooden chairs. From this distance, they appeared to be Native American. I thought it strange that they remained sitting in their chairs until I picked up on the duct tape wound around them, a lot of duct tape.

Beyond them, wingback chairs were positioned in front of a large stone fireplace. The mantel consisted of one massive split log running along the entire width of the fireplace. Above the mantel was a framed painting that looked just like the tattoo I'd seen on the arm of one of the security guys at the Grey Wolf Casino; a war shield with eagle feathers.

Carlos glanced back and saw me staring at the couple bound to the chairs. He raised his glass toward them in a toast, took a sip, then said, "Yeah, can you believe it. This place is all casino money. Five years ago, they were probably living in some shitty government housing and now look at 'em. It's only right they maybe share some of the wealth with the rest of us."

"Hey, look, I know exactly what you're thinking. So just relax, no one got shot here, okay. I just wanted to get their attention. So take a good look, it all just goes to show that if you cooperate, and don't cause any problems, good things can happen. I'm not a mean guy, honest. I'm really not. I just don't need any problems, especially from someone like you, simple as that."

"Besides, maybe look at it this way, just where in the hell are they gonna go all wrapped up like that. See, because they were so nice, I'm actually going to help them out. It's only fitting we take this set of wheels for a ride, you know blow the carbon out, get it moving. Hell, they probably haven't gotten it up much over thirty since they bought the damned thing. I figure we'll be doing them a big favor. Don't you think?" he said, then took a long sip and nodded in satisfaction.

We walked around the split rail fence and over to the Mercedes. Carlos pulled a set of keys from his pocket and pushed a button. The car horn chirped, and the lights blinked twice. Then Carlos said, "Okay, you can hop in."

I moved toward the back door where I could clearly see the little girls sitting in the backseat. They were holding hands, Ava was crying, and Emma looked like she was about ready to.

"Not there, you idiot, my God, what the hell are you thinking. That would be nothing but irresponsible on my part. I can't have those two little innocents in the backseat exposed to someone like you. Here, climb in," he said and then pulled up the trunk of the car.

I looked at the open trunk as Carlos reached in and slid the pink suitcase over to one side. He picked up two vodka bottles and wedged them between the pink suitcase and the inside of the trunk.

"Compliments of our new friends, never know when I'll need a pick me up," he shrugged. "Okay, now in you go, sweetheart. I've made it all nice and comfy for the ride. See, I even have this little suitcase set up so you can use it like a pillow. You can rest your not so pretty little head and take a nap while I do all the work. Come on, get your ass in there." he said.

I stepped up into the trunk and then carefully knelt down. At any moment, I expected Carlos to slam the trunk down on my head, but he actually helped to guide me in then adjusted the suitcase, so I could rest my head on it once I was lying down. I ended up on my side with my knees scrunched up and my head resting on the pink suitcase.

He reached in and pulled one of the vodka bottles out from behind the suitcase and carefully poured close to three inches into his glass and swirled it around. There was barely enough orange juice left to give the drink some color.

I glanced around my quarters and saw what looked like a GPS transponder mounted on the back of the rear seat. I could only hope the thing was working.

Carlos stuffed the vodka bottle back behind the suitcase and stood over me with another idiotic grin plastered across his face. He looked down at me, then laughed and snickered, "Sweet dreams, darling." Just before he slammed the trunk closed and I was left lying in the dark.

I heard the car door open and felt the vehicle jostle ever so slightly as he settled behind the wheel. A moment later, the engine started. I heard him say something to the girls before we started moving. The car rolled slowly backward and stopped for half a moment, then started forward at a moderate speed. After a minute or two, we came to a stop, made a lefthand turn and started to pick up speed.

# Twenty-six

We continued traveling at a fairly steady rate of speed. Once in a while, he seemed to accelerate, and I'd feel a slight shift first to the left and then back again to the right, which I presumed meant we were passing someone. We were traveling and making time, but I didn't have the sense we were speeding. The continual drone from the rear tire next to my head began to make me drowsy.

Laying there in the dark, and hearing only the tires spinning made my sense of time more or less disappear. It could have been an hour or five hours before I felt us making a series of turns. After a few minutes, it sounded like we were traveling on a gravel road. We stopped a short time after that, and the car rocked back and forth, indicating Carlos was climbing out.

A moment later, the trunk opened up. I had to blink a few times in an effort to adjust my eyes as daylight bolted in from the cloudless sky. I closed my eyes for a long moment until my sight recovered.

"How we doing back here?" Carlos asked then reached behind the suitcase for a vodka bottle. He held the bottle out and focused on the label, apparently attempting to read the thing before he mumbled, "Whatever."

He cracked the seal, put the bottle to his lips, and tasted then stood there deep in thought. "Yeah, that should work," he said and nodded like it was a good idea. He poured vodka into his glass until it was maybe half full, then screwed the top back on and stuffed the bottle back behind the suitcase.

From the little I could see, we were in the middle of a forest on some gravel road. There were birch trees, lots of birch trees, no buildings to speak of, and not another vehicle in sight.

"Tell you what I'm gonna do, pal. Because I'm genuinely a nice guy and seeing as how you've behaved yourself for the first part of the journey, I think I might let you drive. I'll just sip, relax, and keep the girls' company in the backseat. Think you can handle that?"

I must have conveyed what I was thinking with my eyes.

"Don't worry. I won't shoot you. I mean, understand me, if you do something stupid, I'll just shoot one of those little brats. After all, you're behind the wheel. So, how's that sound?"

He took a sip and seemed to look around like he was waiting for my reply then he looked down at me and said, "Well?" He suddenly focused on the length of tape across my mouth and said, "Oh, for Christ's sake, will you give me that." Then he reached down, grabbed the end of the tape, and yanked, tearing the length from my face. It made a sound like fabric ripping on an expensive coat.

I gasped and coughed a couple of times. The skin on either side of my mouth felt raw, my lips stung, and for just a brief moment, I wondered if this was what women went through when they got waxed.

"So, you up for it, gonna help us out?" he asked and took another healthy sip from his drink.

"You want me to drive?"

"That's what I just said, Jesus, were you listening?"

"Yeah, I can do that."

"Good, good, here, let me help you," he said, then took a handful of my hair in his fist and pulled me up into a sitting position.

"Ouch, ahhh, God, okay, I'm up, I'm up."

"Calm down, I was just trying to help, you know, lending a hand here. Tell you what, you just turn around, and we'll get that stuff off your wrists," he said and set his glass next to me on the floor of the trunk.

As I turned around, I thought the moment I get this tape off my wrists, I'm going to tear this idiot apart. Then, I'm going to tie him to the front of the car and drive to the nearest police station.

I heard something click behind me as he opened up a knife, and then I felt him cutting through some of the tape on my wrists. There was a definite loosening, but the tape was still holding my wrists together.

"There," he said, picking up his drink glass and taking a couple of steps away from me. "You should be able to get the rest of that tape off if you just pull and twist it. Looks like I really had you bound up pretty good."

I could definitely move my hands and wrists more, and I wiggled and pulled them back and forth until my righthand finally came free. It felt wonderful to begin to get the circulation flowing back into my arms. I took my time pulling all the tape off my lefthand. I rolled my shoulders and turned my head from side to side in an effort to bring the circulation back and get rid of the numbness that had set in.

Carlos had moved a good ten feet from me. He continued to sip his drink while he kept the Sig Sauer trained on my back. "You about ready to climb out, or have you grown attached to lying in the trunk?"

"I can climb out," I said. I groaned as I gingerly stretched first one leg and then the other out of the trunk of the car and carefully stood. I turned from side to side at my waist and felt my spine crackle and pop. "Let me just stretch and walk back and forth for a minute or two and get the blood flowing again. Okay?"

"Move over there and make it fast. You try anything, I promise I'll shoot you first. Then I'll let you watch while I shoot those two little girls, and it will all be your fault. Got it?"

"Yeah, yeah, I get it. I just need to get the blood flowing before I climb behind the wheel, that's all. How

many hours have we been on the road?" I asked as I began walking back and forth, shaking my arms, rolling my
shoulders, getting the kinks out of my neck. It felt wonderful.

"How many hours? Try about forty-five minutes.
How does that sound? You about done wasting my
time?"

"Yeah, I'm ready to drive, let's go."

"Just stay there for a minute," Carlos said. He
reached back into the trunk, pulled the vodka bottle out,
and topped up his glass. He slammed the trunk closed
then said, "Why don't you just walk up past the front of
the car and stand there so you can't do anything stupid."

I walked up to the front of the car and stood on the
gravel road. I continued to roll my shoulders and move
my neck back and forth.

"Move forward a couple more paces," he said.

Once I moved forward, I heard the car door open,
and then the dinging alarm sounded signaling the key
was in the ignition. I heard another door open, and then
Carlos called, "Okay, let's get going, just walk backward
to the driver's door and climb in."

I did as instructed, walking backward and almost
tripping as I reached the driver's door. Carlos was seated
directly behind the driver's seat with little Ava on his
lap. She was holding his glass of vodka with both hands.
Her eyes were wide, and her lower lip was trembling, but
she wasn't crying. He sat smirking with the Sig Sauer
pressed against her side.

"You just make damned sure you stay at the speed limit he said, nothing fancy. Anything happens, or you try anything to draw attention to us, and there'll be trouble back here, got it?"

"Yeah," I nodded. "I got it," I said as I slid behind the wheel. I adjusted the side and rearview mirrors, then started the car and put it in gear. I made a slow 'U' turn until we were headed in the opposite direction.

"Good, now just follow this until you hit pavement, take a left, and it'll take you right back to the freeway in a minute or two. Just remember, we're all watching, so nothing fancy."

We were heading south again on I-35 just a few minutes later. Traffic was light, and the roads were clear. A few miles down the Interstate, I spotted a Minnesota Highway Patrol car parked in the medium. They're impossible to miss, a deep burgundy with white doors and a logo in the shape of the state on the door. Flashing lights are mounted on the top of the vehicle, and just in case you have any doubts, gold letters, all capitals, spell out STATE PATROL on all sides of the vehicle.

All the drivers reacted the same way. Even if they were driving below the posted limit, every car on the road hit their brakes just to be sure, flashing the brake lights for a moment. The truth of the matter is he was probably just sitting there filling out paperwork.

I thought about flashing the headlights or maybe even speeding up to try and signal him in some way. I gave a quick glance in the rearview mirror and caught

Carlos staring back at me. He smiled, winked and continued to stare. I stayed in the righthand lane, and we just drove past not attracting any attention.

"Good boy, very good boy," Carlos said, then sipped.

# Twenty-Seven

Heading south, the traffic seemed to noticeably pick up once we passed the town of Hinckley. The town seemed to serve as the very outer edge for folks who were long-distance commuters going into the twin cities. I continued to check on Carlos in the rearview mirror, and unfortunately, he continued to meet my gaze. Sometimes he smiled. Once in a while, he even winked, but no matter when I looked, he always seemed to be staring back at me.

We were coming into the northern ring of suburbs. From here on in one community flowed into the next. We were just passing the town of Forest Lake when Carlos said, "The road splits up here in a couple of miles I want you to take 35E into St. Paul. I'll give you more directions as we get closer to town."

I watched him in the rearview mirror draining his glass, he gave another one of his satisfied gasps then dropped the empty glass onto the floor of the backseat. He checked me out in the mirror for a long moment then looked over at the girls. They had scooted over to the far side of the backseat, as far away from him as possible, and were still holding each other's hand.

"I know what we should do. How 'bout we all sing a little song. You got one you like?"

Little Ava just stared at the floor and pretended not to hear him. Emma glanced over quickly, shook her head, and then stared straight ahead.

"Okay, suit yourself, but let me just say you two aren't very much fun. Fine with me if you're gonna be that way, I'll just pick something that I like." With that he hummed a note, pretending to gain a perfect pitch or something before he burst into an off-key rendition of Frosty the Snowman.

It was a gorgeous fall day, bright and sunny. The temperature was set at sixty-nine degrees in the car as we sailed down the road doing our best not to listen to idiot Carlos as he forever destroyed any positive thoughts we may have had regarding Frosty the Snowman.

There's something about drunks singing, actually a number of things, that in very short order become unpleasant. It's why I'd given up going to concerts. Pay a hundred and twenty bucks for a ticket and I always end up next to the drunk who plans on singing along with every song. At least at a concert, you could tell the idiot to shut up, call security, or just leave and go to a bar.

None of those options existed driving down the interstate in a stolen Mercedes with a gun pointed at us. I lost count of how many times Carlos sang the only verse he knew. One was too many. He even had the lyrics wrong, singing "stocking cap" instead of "old silk hat." Not that I intended to correct him. When he got to the

"Thumpity, thump, thump" part, he drummed his hands on the back of my seat, supposedly in time. I would have given anything to grab him and hurl him out the door, and still, he continued on.

I noticed a vehicle in the side mirror coming up behind us. It was swinging out into the passing lane, then back into the right lane for a bit, then out again, ducking back and forth. At first, I thought it was an SUV, but the silhouette quickly became all too familiar. A Humvee, black, with lots of chrome and lights mounted on the roof. I watched for a good ten minutes as it continued to swerve in and out of traffic, slowly, but surely gaining on us.

My initial hope was that it was some police vehicle, but the more I watched it in the mirrors, the less that seemed to be a possibility. The zooming in and out of lanes was not the sort of driving an official vehicle would be doing on the interstate. And the lights mounted on the top were for illuminating things, not flashing.

I slowed ever so slightly, hoping Carlos wouldn't notice. He didn't, unfortunately, only because he was on about his thousandth rendition of Frosty. Little Ava had put her hands over her ears in an effort to block out the sound, which only served to encourage Carlos. By now, the lyrics were hopelessly mangled, and in an effort to restart, Carlos was pounding out, literally, the "thumpity, thump, thump" part twice as often. We all had headaches.

A red car behind us gradually picked up the slack and put its left blinker on getting ready to pass, but the Humvee seemed to hang in the passing lane just off its bumper forcing it to stay behind us. Then the Humvee quickly sped up and pulled alongside the Mercedes.

I glanced over and then saw the logo of the Grey Wolf Casino on the passenger door, small world. I thought the figure in the front passenger seat with the laptop computer looked vaguely familiar. He had a long ponytail pulled tightly behind his head, and I suddenly recognized the tattoo on his softball-sized bicep, the shield with eagle feathers hanging from it. At the same time, he casually glanced over at me, and a look of recognition seemed to spread across his face. His eyes widened then his face turned into an evil glare as he focused on the singer in the backseat.

Carlos was in the process of drumming again, singing, "Thumpity, thump, thump. Thumpity, thump, thump. Look at Frosty go."

I mouthed the word "Help" a couple of times, then inclined my head and indicated with my thumb back toward Carlos. For his part, Carlos was still horribly out of tune and pounding away on the back of my seat in full concert mode. I could only hope the guy took note of the gun Carlos was holding on us.

He turned and seemed to say something to whoever was driving and the Humvee suddenly dropped back and then pulled over into the righthand lane. As soon as they

pulled in, the red car behind us zoomed out into the passing lane, gave me a quick glance, then sailed past and
kept on going.

Carlos continued destroying Frosty for another
twelve miles, then suddenly stopped in mid-verse and
sounded almost rational for a brief moment as he gave
me directions. "Okay, you want to take the next exit,
that's Maryland Ave. When you get to the top you can
make a left and go over the bridge then just keep going.
I'll tell you what to do after that."

Mercifully he didn't start singing Frosty again, instead, he just hummed the thing half to himself, at least
up until the thumping part when he suddenly broke out
into the chorus again and started pounding once more
against the back of my seat. Both the girls pressed their
hands back over their ears.

I took the Maryland exit and then watched in the
mirror as the Humvee did the same thing two cars behind
me. I pulled up to the light and waited with my lefthand
blinker on. Just before the red light changed to a green
arrow, the doors on the Humvee flew open, and four
large guys in black T-shirts with white letters that said
SECURITY piled out, at least two of them were carrying
what looked like sawed-off shotguns. I waited for a long
moment hoping they'd get up to our car, but they seemed
to pause briefly questioning the traffic light.

The car behind us leaned on the horn, and Carlos
said, "Hey, come on man, this is a quick light, get your

ass in gear." Then he looked over his shoulder at the car honking behind us.

I pulled ahead just as the light went yellow, the car behind us made the turn then whipped past us, and a middle-aged woman gave me the finger. The guys in the Humvee jumped back in, then screeched through the intersection, running the red light as they followed.

The windows in the Humvee were heavily tinted, and I couldn't see how many people were in the thing. I could only hope it was crammed full, and they were all heavily armed.

I drove up the hill on Maryland and across Payne Avenue. After a few more blocks, Carlos leaned forward in the backseat and said, "Take the next right and keep going." No sooner had we turned onto the side street, then he leaned forward again and asked, "Are they still back there?"

"What?"

"Don't be stupid. Those guys from the Grey Wolf Casino, are they still back there."

"What are you talking about?"

From behind me, I heard the audible click of the hammer on the Sig Sauer. "You're not thinking of getting cute, are you? That Humvee, the one that's been following us for the last forty miles. God only knows how they found us. It's filled with security guys from the Grey Wolf, but you most likely already knew that. So let me ask you again, are they still behind us?"

"Yeah, yes, they are, but they seem to be hanging back by maybe a good block or more."

"Are we going to see mommy soon?" Emma asked.

"I want my mommy," Ava cried.

"Shut up, kid," Carlos growled.

"What do you want me to do? You got any ideas? Want me to try and lose them?" I asked.

"Tell you what, just keep going down this street for a few more blocks, there'll be a building on the righthand side, on the corner. It's brick, four stories. Take your time getting there, and hopefully, they'll keep their distance. I got something to do back here," he said.

I heard him rustle around in the backseat for a moment, and then there was a metallic click just before Emma shouted, "Don't, you're wrecking it. Dev, he's wrecking the seat, he's wrecking it."

She sounded frightened, and when I glanced in the rearview mirror, I saw both the girls staring at Carlos as he shoved his knife into the upper left corner of the backseat and slit the thing, sawing down to the lower right corner. Then he shoved the blade into the upper righthand corner and sawed across the seat again to the lower-left corner. Yellow foam padding puffed out of the ruined seat in the shape of an "X," and Carlos frantically pulled handfuls of foam padding out and cast it aside then reached into the seat for more.

"He's wrecking the car, Dev, he's wrecking the car," Emma shouted. Ava just sat wide-eyed and stared.

She'd moved as far away from Carlos as possible and was almost on top of her sister.

Carlos reached in and felt around, pulling more foam out. I could hear him ripping fabric from the inside of the seat, and I wondered if he had suddenly gotten wise to the GPS transponder attached in the trunk.

"I think I see that brick building on the right coming up. We're about a block away."

"Let me just get hold of this damned thing and, okay, here we go, here we go, come on," he said, then seemed to wrestle something out through the sliced open backseat. He suddenly turned around with a large smile across his face and set the pink suitcase on his lap.

"Keep your foot off the brake pedal until you pull in front of that building," he said, pulling a keyring out of his pocket. "I'm grabbing this little cry baby," he said, dragging Ava across the backseat. "You and bossy better hurry up before they have a chance to get much closer."

With that, I crossed the intersection and Carlos was suddenly out the door with the suitcase and Ava under his arm before the car had come to a stop. He left the door open as they stumbled into the street.

"No, no, no, Emma, Emma," Ava screamed and kicked as Carlos dashed around the back of the car and then up the front steps of the building.

"God damn it, quit kicking, kid, I'm warning you," he screamed. He stood at the entrance, holding the security door open, waiting for us as Ava squirmed in an effort to try and get out from underneath his arm. "Come on, come on, you're taking all day," Carlos screamed.

I slammed the car in park and jumped out from behind the wheel just as the Humvee began to roar down the street toward us. I could hear it accelerating as I grabbed Emma from the backseat, and we charged up the front steps two at a time.

We ran into the building, and Carlos pulled the security door closed. The lock made an audible sound, and Ava squirmed loose from his side and wrapped her arms around my thigh. I heard a screech from out on the street as the Humvee screeched across the intersection then popped into view a half-second before it slammed into the rear of the Mercedes and skidded to a stop.

# Twenty-eight

Carlos directed us down the hallway with the Sig Sauer. "Come on, hopefully, they'll check out my place up on the third floor." Halfway down the hall, he opened the door labeled Laundry Room. The girls and I hurried down some stairs into the basement ahead of him. He pulled the door closed and slid a small deadbolt lock in place. "Keep moving," he shouted just as we heard heavy pounding on the security door up in the hallway behind us.

A moment later, the unmistakable sound of breaking glass and an alarm going off was followed by a lot of shouting and some awfully heavy footsteps that charged down the hallway past the laundry room door and then up the flight of stairs at the far end of the hall.

"I knew it would work. Bastards'll head up to the third floor thinking that's where we went, the dumb shits. Come on, that way," Carlos yelled and patted the little pink suitcase tucked under his arm.

We hurried down a dimly lit hallway. Carlos was in the rear, still waving the Sig Sauer and looking over his shoulder. "Come on, keep moving, keep moving, all the way down to the end."

I held Emma by the hand and carried Ava as we hurried down the hallway. Ava's arms were wrapped tightly around my neck, and her head was buried against my shoulder, I could feel her little body shaking.

"Its okay, Ava, its okay," Emma kept saying to her, all the while grasping my hand tightly.

For her part, Ava seemed to be taking none of the encouragement to heart, and she clung even tighter to my neck as we made our way down the hallway toward the distant open door.

"You know, Carlos. I'm thinking you could make a lot better time if you just went on ahead and left the three of us here. You know, made tracks to get out of here all by yourself," I said.

"You just keep moving, wiseass, and I'll be the one doing all of the thinking around here."

I felt like asking him just how well that plan was working but decided to keep my mouth shut.

The open door at the end of the long hallway led into the laundry room. Three washers and three dryers, all coin-operated stood side by side in the middle of the room. Next to the washers was an old-fashioned laundry tub. It featured two sinks made of concrete sitting on a steel stand. It must have been original to the building, predating World War II by a generation.

The basement walls looked to be almost eight feet high and constructed out of concrete block. They had been painted a glossy white some time ago. The laundry room floors were a dull battleship grey and could have used a good cleaning.

A couple of bare light bulbs with pull chains served to light the room, although at this time of day, more than enough sunlight was streaming through the basement windows, and the bulbs weren't needed. The only piece of furniture in the room was a picnic table pushed up against the wall opposite the clothes dryers.

Next to the picnic table was a wastebasket filled to overflowing with empty plastic containers of laundry detergent, fabric softener, and the occasional handful of dryer lint. It looked like it hadn't been emptied in at least a year.

Four bicycles hung upright from a rack attached with long brackets to the laundry room ceiling. Carlos paused and examined them for a moment then shook his head disgustedly.

"Son of a bitch, this pisses me off. I guess they don't trust anyone, so they went ahead and locked the things up. Now, when I could really use a break, you know hop on one of these things and just pedal away, guess what? I'm screwed. Thanks a lot for nothing," he said and kicked one of the bikes. That started a chain reaction, and they swung back and forth, looking like they might fall off the rack if it weren't for the locks holding them in place.

We suddenly heard two dull reports, one right after the other that sounded an awful lot like shotgun blasts coming from somewhere above us in the building. Emma moved in closer to me.

"Well, there you go, so much for the locks on the door," Carlos said. "Come on, that was our traveling music, we'll head out the backdoor and circle around the building back to the car." He opened the bolt lock on the door leading outside and cautiously peeked out, then quickly waved us forward with the Sig Sauer.

The door opened up to five concrete steps with thick concrete walls on either side. The steps and the walls were painted the same white as the laundry room and led up to ground level. As we stepped outside, I could hear some fairly substantial noise coming from one of the units three stories above us— angry voices and what sounded like lots of dishes being broken.

When Carlos stepped out, he immediately glanced up and seemed to half-smile to himself. "Get up these steps, and we'll go along the side of the building back out to the front. When you get to the corner of the building, hold up and wait for me," he said.

It sounded like everything was crashing and breaking in his apartment up on the third floor, and he moved us forward with another wave of the Sig Sauer. We hurried along the side of the apartment building until we came to the front.

"Hold it right there," Carlos half-whispered from behind as he squeezed past us and peeked out to the front sidewalk.

Apparently, the coast was clear because he gave a wave with the pistol then hurried out toward the Mercedes. A woman who had been walking her dog was standing on the sidewalk with her back to us. She was holding the leash and a blue plastic bag of dog poop in one hand, her cellphone in the other, and completely oblivious to us coming up behind her.

"No, it's a large vehicle, black, with a Grey Wolf Casino sign on the door. It looks like some hot rod or something and appears to have smashed into this Mercedes. What? No, I'm not seeing anyone around, but there's broken glass and bits and pieces of car all over the street. This big black vehicle is blocking part of the cross street and—"

As Carlos came up behind her, the little white dog began to bark. Before she had a chance to turn around and see us, he snatched the phone from her hand and said, "Wrong number," to whomever she had been talking to. Then he shoved her phone into his front pocket.

"What in God's name do you think you're doing? Have you lost your mind? I just happened to be talking to the police for your information. You can't do that, give me back that phone, this instant," she shrieked then stood with her chin jutted out and her bottom lip trembling, glaring at Carlos.

"Get the hell out of here, lady."

"Now you listen here," she started in, but then focused on the pistol as Carlos slowly raised it and pointed it directly at her face. Her eyes grew wide, and she was suddenly very quiet.

"I think you better listen to him," I said, trying to warn her off before she became a casualty.

"Well, I never," she said, then yanked the leash, and the little furry white dog on the far end leaped up into her arms. She began to march down the sidewalk, lecturing with the dog in her arms and still holding the blue plastic bag. "Well, you can just rest assured we'll…."

Carlos aimed his pistol at the rear tire of the Humvee and fired. The round punctured the tire, and it quickly deflated, giving off an evil hiss. The woman with the dog screamed, tossed the dog and the blue plastic bag up in the air, and took off running down the street. The dog took off at a perpendicular angle and ran across the street to a female lab stretched out on the front lawn.

Carlos gave a satisfied smile as the woman disappeared down the street, then waved us into the Mercedes and said, "You just better hope this thing starts, and you can get us the hell out of here, man."

# Twenty-nine

Emma held her little sister's hand while Carlos stood off to the side and cursed us for not moving faster. I ushered the girls into the backseat and then ran around the front of the car, checking the wheels as I went. The rear of the car appeared to have been virtually destroyed when the Humvee slammed into it. The trunk was buckled, the taillights were broken, and the rear window was cracked, but when I put it in drive to pull away from the curb, it responded.

As we pulled away from the curb and headed down the street, I glanced in the rearview mirror and saw bits and pieces of debris bouncing off the pavement. Carlos seemed to heave a sigh of relief.

I don't know if it was by design or just the way it worked out, but the girls were seated on the side Carlos had sliced up and desperately clung to the remnants while he had the one comfortable rear seat. He turned around and stared out the back window looking for any activity in the street behind us.

I watched in the sideview mirror as two large looking guys suddenly emerged from the building and ran out into the street. One of them raised a shotgun and fired, but it didn't seem to have any effect. I sped up, all the same, causing a hubcap from a rear-wheel to fly off and bounce across the street into a parked car.

"What's up with those Grey Wolf Casino guys? What's their problem?" I asked and then suddenly remembered the transponder mounted in the trunk.

"Bunch of sore losers, I guess. I just can't figure out how they found us. I mean, what are the odds?"

I wanted to tell him the odds were about a hundred percent with the tracking device in the trunk. I could only hope their Humvee would be able to start, and they'd catch up with us. "I don't think they're after you because you won too much."

"Man, what a waste. I met this chick, and we ended up there. Let's just say she turned out to be a lot more work than I wanted to put in, and she did nothing except bring me bad luck at the tables."

"Did you skip out on your room charge or something?"

"I didn't actually skip out. I just left. I figured as long as that chick was such a pain, she could pay the damned thing. And, well, then there was that little unscheduled withdrawal that I made?"

I flashed him a look in the rearview mirror. "Unscheduled withdrawal?"

"Those security jerk-offs hassled me because this bitch was acting like a royal pain in the ass. This is after they banned me from the roulette wheel and then the blackjack tables. So much for nice customer service."

"Anyway, I just wanted another drink, and this chick was doing nothing but bitching, so I figured, screw this, and I just left. Who'd hang around for more of that? I sure as hell don't need that kinda shit. On the way out, I stopped by the cashiers' window, and they were doing a shift change or something, not paying too much attention, and so I just helped myself."

"You mean, you robbed them?"

"I suppose that's one way to look at it. Another might be I just took back some, not all, but a percentage of what they took from me. Next time maybe they'll think twice before they decide not to give me a chance to win it all back."

"How big of a percentage?"

"I haven't had time to count it, but I'm guessing about ninety maybe ninety-five percent. I just can't figure out how in the hell they got on to us down here and in this car."

"Maybe start with taking the girls, then of course, the car you left in Two Harbors, my car actually. I don't know, maybe fueling up and fleeing in the boat might have had something to do with it. Obviously, that guy in the harbor called the cops, remember the helicopter? Don't forget the couple who own this car, you tied them up and left them. You said they were tribal members, getting checks from the casino, right? You start putting all that together, and it starts to add up, Carlos. You've left a pretty interesting trail and, and well as long as we're on the subject, there's something else."

"Yeah, what's that?"

"The name Tubby Gustafson mean anything to you?"

"Tubby? What the hell do you know about Tubby?" Carlos shrieked, and the color seemed to drain from his face.

"You didn't just happen to make an uninvited stop at one of his card games the night before last, did you? You a Batman fan?"

"How the hell do you know about that? Not that I did it or anything, just more of a hypothetical kind of question."

"Well, someone used my car to rob Tubby. Let me tell you, he's not all that happy about it, and you were the last person seen driving that vehicle."

"Yeah, but how does he know it was even me?"

"You wore a Batman mask, right?"

A shocked look washed over his face.

"I'm here to tell you, Carlos, Tubby really hates Batman. I mean, he *hates* him with a passion. Those casino guys, they're like dealing with little leaguers compared to what Tubby's got out on the streets."

"Oh hell, this really changes things," Carlos said, and I could see him trying to think. Whatever he came up with, the odds were now definitely stacked against him.

"What it really changes is, Tubby isn't the sort of guy to give up. He'll keep looking until he finds you. And, sorry to say, but he's not going to be satisfied with just getting his money back. He's going to want you, too. Not just a piece, Carlos, he's going to want all of you. You know what I'd do if I were you, Carlos?"

"What's that?"

"I'd drop the girls and me off on this next corner up here with that pink suitcase, and then I would just head out of town. Somewhere you've never been, somewhere he'll never think of looking. And then I'd never darken the streets of St. Paul again, ever."

"I knew it. I figured you'd want the cash."

"Really? I tell you what, if you think it will help or if it makes you feel any better you can go ahead and keep the damned cash, Carlos I really don't care. But get your ass out of town. Okay? You drop the girls and me off. By the time we talk to anyone, you'll be long gone, anyway. How does that sound?"

"I got an even better idea, two ideas as a matter of fact. First, you can just shut the hell up and second, take a right at the stoplight up there."

# Thirty

Carlos had us heading west on I-94. He turned around and looked out the rear window about every thirty seconds to see if we were being followed. We passed within a half-mile of my house at one point, not that I volunteered that information to him. I pulled off the interstate at the Snelling Ave exit then headed south down Snelling past Grand Ave.

He took the phone he'd stolen from that lady with the little white dog from his front pocket and dialed a number. After a very long moment, he said, "Hey, wake up, you looking to party? No, it's Carlos, remember? Who the hell is Donny? I could be, say maybe about five minutes. Well, I might have a surprise for you. See you then."

He had me take a right onto St. Clair then another right two blocks later into a neighborhood known locally as Tangle Town due to all the curved streets winding through that section of town.

A minute later we pulled in front of the ugliest house on the block, a smaller, story and a half stucco residence that except for the trash bags next to the front door looked abandoned. It was painted a dingy grey with peeling white trim. Given the area, the house had probably been built before the First World War and had been ugly ever since. The grass should have been cut two or three weeks ago, and the front hedge should have been torn out two or three years ago.

There was a blank space next to the front door where one of the numbers in the four-digit address had fallen off. What was supposed to be a "9" in the address was hanging upside down and looked like a "6." The front window had six panes, five of which were glass, and the sixth held a piece of cardboard.

"You, bossy, get out of the backseat, and come with me, hurry up, now," Carlos said to Emma.

I turned and looked at her over my shoulder. The girls were still holding one another's hand.

"It's okay, I'll watch Ava, you go ahead, Emma."

"I got a much better idea, why don't you give me those car keys and then get the hell out of the car and get over here as well. We're all going in together. Just one big happy family," Carlos said, then pulled the pink suitcase out and said, "Come on, get moving here."

I tossed the keys out the door to Carlos. Emma didn't look too sure, but Carlos was already pulling her out of the backseat. For a brief moment, I thought about running away, but we wouldn't have a chance to make it more than a few feet before he'd start shooting. I climbed out and lifted Ava from the back seat.

"Tell you what, reach into that trunk, and pull out those bottles I got in there. It usually works better if I show up with refreshments."

I reached through the backseat Carlos had slit open and felt around for the bottles. I almost had to crawl into the trunk before I felt them lying in a far corner. I grabbed them and then pretended to continue searching while I pulled the GPS Transponder off the rear of the backseat and shoved it into my pocket.

"Take the kids up to the door and knock, the doorbell's broken. You'll probably have to give it a good pounding, she's not big on visitors, and she's probably been partying for a couple of days. I'll be right behind you."

The front door was probably very nice at one time, maybe back a century ago. It was in desperate need of some serious cleaning and refinishing. The area around the doorknob was coated with twenty or thirty years of grime, and the doorknob itself had been turned so many times the brass finish had worn off long ago. Now it was just a cold, dark piece of lifeless steel. The lower third of the door was devoid of any finish and was severely warped where the veneer hadn't already fallen off after decades of exposure to the elements.

There was a small leaded window in the pattern of a stained glass flower in the upper portion of the door, so you could look out and see who was at the door. It was probably charming in its day, unfortunately now it was taped over with a cheap piece of plastic because half the pieces of stain glass were missing. An ancient yellowed window shade, curled and with a ragged tear along the righthand side, covered the small window from the inside.

Carlos was right. The doorbell didn't work. In fact, there wasn't a doorbell. Three cloth-covered wires extended out a hole where the doorbell once sat. I stood on the poured concrete front steps and knocked politely on the door.

"I said pound on the damned thing, or she won't hear you. This hour she's probably already half in the bag if she hasn't passed out altogether in front of the TV or isn't singing along with Pink Floyd."

I pounded on the door a half dozen times. A moment later, the yellowed shade was lifted, and a pair of bloodshot eyes stared out at me. They seemed to come alive once they were able to focus on Carlos. A couple of locks clicked on the far side of the door, and a moment later, the door creaked opened. A cloud of stale, stuffy air drifted out over us, and everyone recoiled.

"Carlos, when did you get out?"

"Frannie, we just talked on the phone a few minutes ago."

"Oh yeah, I kinda remember, maybe. That was you? So you finished the rehab?"

"I just walked away, Frances, that dull life ain't for me. Hey, how about letting us in," he said, lifting up his two vodka bottles like a prized fish catch, then he pushed me from behind with the Sig Sauer.

Frances stepped back as she pulled the door open and, at the same time, blew a cloud of blue smoke up toward the ceiling. She looked a good fifteen years older than Carlos, but then again, what I suspected might be the lifestyle could have added to that. She was in a ratty housedress with a fistful of Kleenex stuffed in one of the pockets and a pair of grungy blue fuzzy slippers on her feet. Her hair was limp and greasy and hadn't seen a brush or shampoo in quite some time. She had a good inch of grey roots showing after the last home dye job. Her nose was chapped and raw, and she rubbed it with the crumpled Kleenex she held in her fist.

"What the hell is all this?" she asked, indicating the girls and me. Then she took another drag from her cigarette, let loose with a raspy cough, and flicked the inch-long ash toward us.

Ava wrapped her arms a little tighter around my neck, and Emma pulled in closer to my side, holding my hand tightly. I looked over at Carlos, waiting for him to explain his way out of this.

"Kind of a complication, but nothing you have to worry your pretty little head about. Look at what I brought you, here take these," Carlos said and handed the vodka bottles over to her.

"Oh boy, aren't we gonna have some fun," Frances giggled.

Carlos set the pink suitcase on top of the dirty plates and bowls scattered across the coffee table in the living room. He shoved an overflowing ashtray off to the side and set a bong down on the floor.

He looked up at Frances with a large grin, then slowly pulled the zipper around the outside of the suitcase, lifted the top and stepped back. "Check it out, Frannie."

She leaned in to take a peek and a look of shocked surprise spread across her face, after a long moment, she shouted, "What the hell?" She looked back and forth from the currency crammed in the suitcase to Carlos standing there smirking. "What in the hell is all this? You rob a bank or something?"

"Let's just say I placed a couple of bets and managed to get a little lucky. Hell of a lot better than wasting my time in rehab, don't you think."

"This calls for a celebration," Frances said and gave Carlos a big hug. "Alright, you just wait here, and I'll be right back."

She hurried through a large oak archway into the dining room where the table was covered with a pile of laundry, I guessed dirty. A mound of grocery store circulars and unopened mail littered the end of the dining room table closest to us. Some of the mail had spilled off the table, and a second pile was growing on the floor. She set the vodka bottles on the table next to the pile of laundry.

A built-in oak cabinet in the far wall was littered with bottles and glasses. More than one of the glasses had liquid in them and a few cigarette butts. She opened one of the cabinet doors and pulled out two stemmed glasses, the kind for martinis. She blew some dust off the glasses and picked up a plastic vodka bottle from off the top of the cabinet and filled a glass. She emptied the bottle in the process, only halfway filling the second glass.

"Damn it," she said, then tilted her head to the side, so the smoke from her cigarette mostly avoided her eyes. She cracked the seal on another plastic bottle, unscrewed the top, and proceeded to finish filling the glass.

"Here's to our newfound success," she said and handed Carlos a glass. They clinked their glasses together in a toast and drank. Carlos took a large gulp, Frances pretty much downed her entire glass.

She licked her lips, looked at the glass and emptied what little remained, wiped the back of her hand across her mouth, then looked at the girls and me and said, "And just what the hell is all this?"

"Just a little bit of baggage, but nothing you need to worry your pretty little head about. They'll be out of the way."

# Thirty-one

Frances smiled, ran her fingers through her greasy hair, and tugged at her housedress apparently in an effort to make a more stunning impression.

"What I'd like to do, Frannie is maybe pull your car out front, put that wreck of my Mercedes in your garage, just for overnight, if that's okay. I'm just a bit worried about leaving it on the street while we get reacquainted. Then if you can fit it in, maybe the two of us will have a little celebration and plan our trip. Sound good to you?"

"I've never really needed a reason to celebrate," she said matter of factly. "But, a trip sounds wonderful, let me get you my car keys," she said then staggered back into the dining room and poured herself a fresh drink before she wandered off sipping and in search of her car keys.

"Hey, look, Carlos, just a thought. We could just walk out of here, the girls and I. You know, not get in the way. You and your friend, Frances, can party up a storm to your hearts' content, and you won't have to worry about us. We're not going to tell a soul, I promise."

Carlos shook his head and said, "Believe me, I ain't worried. I got a plan that'll work just fine."

Frances staggered back into the dining room a few minutes later with an empty glass, poured herself a fresh drink, and said, "I just can't remember where I put those damned car keys."

"Maybe try and think where you went last time you left the house."

"Where I went?" she said and gulped from her glass. "Well, let's see, I just drove to the liquor store, of course. I think that was yesterday or was it last week?" A light suddenly seemed to go on in her head. "I know just the spot," she said, then took a couple more gulps almost draining her glass and pushed through the swinging door that led to her kitchen.

She was flying back through the swinging door a moment later with the car keys and an empty glass. She stopped to pour a refill in the dining room while talking to Carlos over her shoulder.

"As soon as you said that, I remembered. I'd just gone to stock up the other day. I found this place down on West Seventh that opens at eight in the morning. I always figure what the hell, I'm usually up anyway. Plus, they don't judge, you know? I know I'm a drunk, hell, I like it, beats the hell out of writing dissertations."

She set the plastic bottle on the dining room table next to the pile of dirty laundry then proceeded to knock the bottle over. Fortunately it was capped. She took a healthy sip just to fortify herself for the ten-foot walk into the living room and then headed toward us.

"No wonder I couldn't find the damned things," she said, handing the keys over to Carlos. "I hung them up on the key hook right next to the back door. God, I can't even remember when that was," she said and then looked like she was trying to think.

Carlos forced a laugh and said, "It really doesn't matter, the important thing is you got them. Let me just escort our guests to your basement, and then I'll bring your car around."

Frances poured down the rest of her drink and said, "Here, mix me another before you do that, will you, sweetie?"

Carlos hadn't taken a sip since the initial toast, and I'd lost count of Frances's intake. She was slurring her words, and she seemed to be oblivious to her housedress coming undone. She fired up another cigarette as Carlos marched off to the dining room to get her a refill. She blew a cloud of smoke toward the ceiling, coughed a smoker's hack, and staggered a couple of steps before she looked down at Emma and said, "Now what's your name, little honey?"

Emma looked at her but didn't say anything. Mercifully Carlos returned, and Frances refocused her attention on the fresh drink.

"Come on, you guys can take it easy downstairs, right through the kitchen door," Carlos said, then waved the Sig Sauer. I carried Ava and directed Emma ahead of me, although she wasn't about to let go of my hand.

We pushed through the swinging door past a sink overflowing with dirty dishes, four partially-filled pans that looked like they contained science experiments sat on the burners of the stove. A half dozen empty Lean Cuisine boxes were scattered on top of a pile of uno-pened mail. Three more empty boxes lay on the floor.

There was an overflowing wastebasket in front of the kitchen sink, and a couple of overflowing trash bags sat on the floor next to the wastebasket. A built-in kitchen nook affair was littered with more dirty plates holding half-eaten food, dirty paper plates, and another empty vodka bottle.

What had once been a box of vanilla ice cream sat on the corner of the kitchen counter. Based on the melted ice cream that had leaked out of the container, run down the cabinet doors and pooled onto the floor, the thing must have been ignored for the better part of a week

"It's really stinky in here," Emma said, looking up at me. Then she took her free hand and plugged her nose.

"Yeah, you might say cooking and cleaning aren't really her strongest attributes," Carlos said, then looked at me with a grin, winked, and said, "Fortunately, she's got some other skills."

He directed us to the basement stairs and turned on the light as the girls and I made our way down the steps. "I'm gonna give this to Frances," he said, indicating the

Sig Sauer. "So don't do anything stupid, I'll be back in about two minutes."

Then he locked the door behind us. It sounded like he wedged something up against the door, probably a chair, and a minute later, I could hear him talking to Frances.

"Cool," she said, and then I heard some thumping against the basement door like she was leaning against it. "'Fore you go, sweetie, top-up my little drinky-poo please," she slurred.

I could follow his footsteps overhead into the dining room, then a few moments later back out to the kitchen where Frances waited.

"I don't want you going down to the basement, just wait right here until I come back. I'll just be a minute."

"No longer than that, or you'll ruin the mood," she giggled, and then I heard the back door close.

There wasn't much to see in the dim basement. Three piles of laundry, one larger than the next, were mounded on the floor in front of the washer. A number of empty boxes and a half dozen more trash bags that looked like they'd been in the basement for quite a while were piled alongside the wooden steps. The remnants of an old bicycle missing a front tire that looked like it probably hadn't been touched in a decade was crammed behind the washing machine. Along one wall, a number of cardboard boxes were stacked three or four high, the bottom boxes all looked like they'd been sitting in water and the entire stack seemed to lean precariously toward the floor.

Despite the fact that the basement was dank, dark, and smelled of mold, it was still a marked improvement over that biohazard of a kitchen upstairs. I checked the basement windows, but they had all been locked and then screwed into place in their wooden frames. We sat down and leaned against the wall as far away from the dirty laundry and the trash bags as we could get. I pulled the girls in close to me, and we all drifted off to sleep.

Occasionally I woke up from the two-person party going on overhead, music, laughing, along with periods of intermittent rhythmic thumping on the floor. I could only hope it meant the two of them were dancing.

# Thirty-two

I popped awake the moment I heard the lock snap open on the basement door. Carlos cautiously stepped halfway down the basement stairs and peered into the distant corner where we had settled. The girls were still sound asleep.

"Time for us to get going, come on sleeping beauty, rise, and shine."

"Here's an idea, why don't you leave us and take off, lock the door again if you're worried about us calling the cops. By the time we get out, you can be long gone," I said.

"You know, I'm getting more than a little tired of your great ideas. If you'll recall, there's a certain sense of insurance that those two bring to the party. No, I think it will work better for me if you all come along, so get off your ass, wake those two up, and let's get going. Come on, move."

I shook Emma awake, Ava was having a tougher time of it, and I carried her. She snuggled into my shoulder and seemed to fall back asleep. We climbed the basement stairs back up into the kitchen. Emma was behind me and still not fully awake. Once we stepped into the kitchen, she plugged her nose and tried not to look at the mess. I couldn't blame her. We rushed past the trash bags, the melted container of ice cream, the overflowing sink, the nook piled high with dirty dishes and used paper plates, and hurried into the dining room.

The coffee table lay scattered across the floor in a number of pieces, looking like some giant had smashed it with a stomp of his foot. Broken plates and dishes were scattered around, all of it covered with the ashes from the once overflowing ashtray. Bits of pizza and discarded food were ground into the already filthy carpet.

Frances was laid out on the floor, more or less spread eagle, in a rather unladylike pose. Her wretched housedress had been rolled up into a ball and discarded in a distant corner. She held an empty stemmed glass in her hand and was awfully still. I was afraid she might be dead.

Carlos stood across the room from her, holding the suitcase. "She was dancing on top of the coffee table and it just all of a sudden broke into little pieces. That kind of brought the party to a close. Too bad, I really liked the song too, the Ramones," he said, sounding more than a little disappointed.

"Is she okay?" I asked.

He picked up the discarded housedress from the corner and threw it across the room in Frances's direction. It landed on her face and half-covered her shoulders. She snorted a few times, rolled over on her side, and began snoring.

"That's not good," Emma said more to herself than anyone else. She made a disgusted face, and we headed out the door.

"Just like before, I want the girls in back with me, you'll drive. Put them in the backseat and then step out in front of the car," Carlos said.

"You know if you'd just stop and think, you'd…."

"I got a much better idea," Carlos said. "You just stop. Don't think. I don't want to hear another damned word."

I was about to say something, but after the look he gave me, I stopped. The words were on the tip of my tongue, and if I stuck it out, he could have read them.

"Good idea, just shut your mouth and keep quiet. Load them into the backseat, and I'll drop the keys out the window once I'm in," Carlos said.

I opened the rear door on a creamy colored Scion, and Emma climbed in. I pushed newspapers, bags, another plastic vodka bottle, and some articles of clothing onto the floor of the backseat, then set Ava, still asleep, in the seat next to Emma. I buckled both of them up and closed the door on their side.

The Scion looked like an industrial shipping container on wheels, basically just your average, ugly, rectangular box with no charm and four wheels. The sideview mirror on the passenger side had been torn off, a jagged hole in the side of the door served as the only reminder of what was once there. A long, deep scrape tinged with red paint from someone else's vehicle ran along the right front quarter panel. The front bumper and the headlight on the passenger side were completely missing. The jagged plastic edges looked like something had just bitten them off.

The rear tire on the passenger side of the car was obviously the spare and therefore, only good for about fifty miles. Someone had sprayed graffiti in black paint along the rear of the car, but it was illegible.

"Nice set of wheels, Carlos, not. Where'd you ever meet this Frances woman, anyway?"

"I took a literature course from her. She's a college professor, or well at least she was when I first met her, 'course that was before she tanked. Hadn't seen her for a few years, and then we linked up in one of my rehab visits. Pretty good chance she won't even remember we were here and sure as hell won't recall what happened to her car. I guess it's just another benefit to the idea of being sober only occasionally. Small world, ain't it?"

"Amazingly small."

"Why don't you just go ahead and step out in front of this thing before I climb in back," Carlos said.

I walked about five feet in front of the Scion and stood looking up and down the street at the nice houses. I could hear birds chirping and the flow of traffic from busy Fairview Avenue running just behind us. With the exception of Frances's house, the neighborhood was lovely and quaint. It was probably a pretty safe bet none of the neighbors dared consider the realities hidden just behind her closed door.

"All right," Carlos said just before he tossed the car keys past me into the street. Then he opened the door and slid in next to Emma.

I picked up the keys and climbed in behind the wheel. Two half-empty coffee cups rested in the console. They'd been sitting there long enough to have mold growing on the surface of both of them. The ashtray was overflowing, and at no surprise, another empty plastic vodka bottle lay on the floor in front of the passenger seat.

"Hey, no offense, Carlos, but I'd say your pal Frances was hiding behind the door when they were passing out basic cleaning skills. It's been quite a while since I've run into anyone who's as big a slob as she is."

Carlos laughed and said, "Yeah, but like I told you, she has her own unique set of skills."

I really didn't care to contemplate Frances's particular *unique* skill set. "So, where to?"

# Thirty-three

Carlos gave me a trendy address. Actually, he didn't give me an address, he just said, "The Peabody."

The Peabody, as everyone knows, is a building housing very exclusive condos built along the bluff overlooking the juncture where the Minnesota River flows into the Mississippi. It's a gated area, positioned at about a forty-five-degree angle to the Mississippi and looking upriver. The view from The Peabody extends for a mile across a state park to historic Fort Snelling sitting on a distant bluff. Everyone in The Peabody is extremely impressed with themselves.

"You know it?" Carlos asked.

"Yeah, I've been there a time or two. Who do you know there?"

He didn't bother to respond but just looked out the window as I drove around the corner and we fled Frances's hovel. The most direct route would be to head toward the river and Shepard Road, the four lane that ran through town along the Mississippi.

"Do you even know where in the hell you're going? You're heading the wrong way," Carlos said a few minutes later.

"Yeah, as a matter of fact, I do know where I'm going. I'm heading this way because we're going to the drive-thru at McDonald's. We're about a mile away."

"McDonald's?" Carlos asked.

"McDonald's," the girls screamed in unison.

"Hey, pal. These kids haven't had a thing to eat since they were on that damned boat. They're hungry, I'm starving, so we're going to McDonald's. A little something solid to soak up the liquid diet you've been on isn't such a bad idea, either. And by the way, you're buying."

"I'm warning you, you try anything funny, and it'll be the last thing these two ever see. Do we understand each other?"

"Relax, I get it, has anyone caused you any problems? We've done exactly what you want, but you have to feed them, come on. I'd say they more than put up with enough BS from you in the last twenty-four hours."

"I want a happy meal," Emma said.

"I want my mommy," Ava said, but she didn't cry.

"Okay, we'll go to McDonald's, the drive-thru. You two don't say anything, got it? And you stay on the straight and narrow, Haskell."

The girls nodded and actually looked happy for a brief moment. I pulled into the McDonald's across from the old Schmidt Brewery. We hit a lull, and I was able to drive right up to the speaker and place our order.

"Good morning, may I take your order please."

I felt like saying get this idiot with the gun out of the backseat. "Two Happy Meals, two fish sandwiches, a large strawberry shake, what are you gonna have, Carlos?"

"A Big Mac, double cheeseburger and a large shake."

"What flavor on the shake?" I asked.

"Chocolate."

"You got that?" I asked into the speaker.

The woman repeated our order, then said, "Your total is twenty-six-fourteen, please pull ahead to the first window."

"Jesus, that's a lot of dough," Carlos said as I pulled ahead.

"Hey, man, come on, you're holding a suitcase full of cash, which by rights actually belongs to a lot of very unhappy people. I think, under the circumstances, you can afford to buy the kids a Happy Meal."

I heard the suitcase unzip behind me, and a moment later, Carlos handed two twenties over my shoulder.

"Twenty-six-fourteen," the girl with the headset said at the first window. She looked like a high school kid, and she smiled. She was the first pleasant person I'd seen in almost two days. Then she just stared, taking in the purple bruises along the side of my face.

"Keep the change," I said and began to coast toward the next window.

"What the, are you crazy? No one tips at McDonald's. That was my money you just gave away," Carlos said. He turned around and looked out the rear window. Just as I was about to reach back and grab him, he turned back and smiled at me. He held the Sig Sauer in his hand with the barrel casually pointed directly at little Ava sitting next to him. His finger was on the trigger. He raised his eyebrows, smiled, and said, "So, do you really want to try it?"

I looked at him for a moment, then turned forward and pulled to a stop at the next window. A moment later, a woman handed two large bags to me. Next, she picked up a tray holding our four drink cups from the counter alongside her. "Thanks for choosing McDonald's. Have a nice day," she said and just stared at my face.

I passed the bags with the Happy Meals back to Emma, "Here you go, girls."

"She looked at you funny," Emma said.

I placed my Fillet-o-Fish sandwiches on the passenger seat and tossed the bag over my shoulder to Carlos. I handed the drinks, one at a time back to the girls. Once they were settled, I passed the chocolate shake back to Carlos.

I wished there was some way I could spit in his shake, but it didn't seem to be an option. I pulled the two moldy coffees out of the cup holders on the console and tossed them on the floor of the passenger seat. The coffee slowly soaked into the pile of trash on the floor.

No one spoke as we feasted on McDonald's, and I headed up Shepard Road along the Mississippi toward The Peabody. Carlos was the first one to finish. He made a loud slurping sound, sucking up the final drop of his chocolate shake. He dropped the empty cup onto the floor, tilted his head back and gave a loud, satisfying belch. The girls gave him a strange look then glanced toward one another, sending a signal with their eyes.

# Thirty-four

We pulled into the private road that led to The Peabody a few minutes later. The road was more of a curvy pathway lined with vintage street lights. A sidewalk ran along either side of the road, and neatly trimmed hedges wound in between maple trees that were in the process of just beginning to turn scarlet. I stopped at the security gate where a keypad was mounted on a brick pillar right next to a camera.

"Punch in zero seven zero one seven four," Carlos said.

I looked at him in the rearview mirror.

"It's the security code," he said then repeated the numbers once I lowered the window.

I pressed the buttons on the keypad, pressed enter, and the gate immediately swung open.

"Head around to the right," he said. "There's two garage doors. The green door leads to the underground parking. You can pull in down there."

I followed another curvy, tree-lined road up to the green garage door marked entrance and pulled alongside another Keypad.

"Just input the same code as before," Carlos said.

"Give it to me again."

"You're kidding."

"Do you want to get in? I'm not kidding. If you want to get in you'll have to give me the code again."

"No wonder you're a PI, God," Carlos scoffed then gave me the code, again.

The door rose, and I pulled down a short ramp.

"Straight ahead then a right at the end, you can pull into spot five-eleven."

I drove to the far end of the parking ramp, actually the length of building past some very nice cars and a lot of open spaces. As parking areas go, it was one of the cleanest I'd ever been in. The floor had been sealed with a glossy coating and looked like it might be washed fairly regularly. Not so much as a drop of oil anywhere.

Once I made the turn, the five-eleven parking space was just a couple of rows ahead of us against the wall. The numbers were stenciled in black on the concrete wall and on the floor as well. The parking spot was almost right next to the elevator door.

"All right, now we're going to take the elevator up to where we're staying tonight, I want everyone to just stare at the floor, don't look up. Got it?" Carlos said.

Both girls nodded.

"You got it, Haskell?"

I nodded.

"Then say so, damn it."

"I heard you, don't look up."

"Much better. Okay, everyone out, and we'll take the elevator to a very nice place."

"When can we see mommy?" Ava said.

"Pretty soon, if you do what you're told. Can you do that?"

Emma nodded, and Ava just stared at her feet.

After a moment, Carlos said, "Come on, get going." Then he inclined his head toward the elevator.

I lifted Ava up and then put my hand out for Emma to grab onto. Carlos clutched his pink suitcase. We waited for no more than half a minute before the elevator arrived.

As the door opened, Carlos said, "Remember, just look at the floor, watch your feet, everyone watch your feet."

I suppose it was fortunate that no one got on the elevator with us. We rose uninterrupted up to the fifth floor, staring at our feet the entire time. When the doors opened, Carlos said, "Okay, take a right down the hall. It's the last door on the right, Haskell. Bossy, you follow them. I'll be right behind all of you."

The hall had thick, plush beige carpet. The walls were painted an off white and illuminated by soft lights embedded in the ceiling, Five-eleven was the third door on the right at the far end of the hall.

"You just move back a few feet," Carlos said to me, taking out a set of keys. "Bossy, you stand in front of him." He pointed to where he wanted us to stand, Ava seemed to have fallen back asleep on my shoulder. I

stepped away from the door, and Emma positioned herself in front of me. Carlos unlocked the door, then
stepped aside and waved us in.

The unit was spacious, with ten-foot ceilings and
walls painted a neutral color. Elaborate white trim surrounded the doors and windows with a thick, eight-inch
high baseboard running around the bottom of the walls.
Thick oriental rugs covered the polished wooden floors.
An entire wall of windows looked upriver over the
treetops of the state park. The sun was low in the sky,
not quite setting, although it would be in a matter of
about forty-five minutes. The windows faced west, and
upon closer examination, one of them was actually a
door that led to a balcony. I immediately thought if I
could only get Carlos out on the balcony, I might be able
to push him off.

"Don't even think about it," Carlos said as if he was
reading my mind. "No one is going out on the balcony.
We're just going to take it easy here for the night. I've
got some planning to do."

"You don't mind me saying, every minute you hang
around this town is burning precious time. They've got
to be tightening the net, man. Why don't you just take
your little pink suitcase, hop in that lousy car, and head
for the hills?"

"You'd like that, wouldn't you?"

"Not a matter of what I'd like. I just don't want these
two in some intense situation, that's all. I promise I'll

give you a twenty-four-hour head start. I won't call anyone, won't report you, nothing."

"Mmm-hmm, sounds like a great opportunity, not.
You must think I'm pretty stupid, Haskell. You'd be on
the phone before I was two steps out the door."

"I wouldn't, Carlos, really. No offense, but right
now, I'd love it if you fled the scene and just abandoned
us here. If it makes you feel any better, go ahead and tie
me up. If there's a phone here, take it with you. I don't
care. I'm just suggesting it would be better for all of us,
yourself included if you just got out of here."

"Well, maybe I've got a plan, already," he said, but
in a way that made me think he didn't have a clue.

"Sure you do, that's why you brought us here."

There was a fireplace on one wall with four framed
photographs, high school graduation photos; three boys
and a girl. One of the boys looked like an awfully young,
baby faced Carlos.

"Let me guess. This is your folks' place? What?
Are they up at the lake or just out for dinner? Gee, how
clever, bringing us here. The cops would never think of
checking for you in your parent's condo, would they?
I'm sure your folks will be thrilled when they find out
what you've done."

"Maybe you should just shut up for your own good."

"Look, man. We're all tired, exhausted, why don't
you—?"

"Why don't you just shut the hell up is what you
should do. Since you're all so tired, maybe all three of

you should just lie down on the floor. Go on, you heard me. Get down on the floor, right in front of the fireplace. Come on, do it, Haskell."

I helped the girls get down on the floor. Ava groaned a little, but never fully woke up. If she snuggled any closer to me, she would be inside my pocket. Emma lay down on the other side of me, then grabbed my hand, and snuggled up against me.

Carlos walked over to some exotic looking marble-topped buffet. He pulled the center drawer open and took out a couple of white extension cords. "Not that I don't trust you, Haskell, but well, I don't," he laughed. "You just stay down there and stretch out so I can tie this around your ankles. I don't want you getting any stupid ideas about turning into some hero in the middle of the night."

I stretched out on the floor, and Carlos wrapped one of the extension cords around my ankles then tied a knot in the thing. When he'd finished, he pulled on the cord a couple of times to make sure it was tight then said, "Roll over on your stomach and put your hands behind your back."

"Oh come on, man, not this again. You gotta be kidding me. I'm not gonna be able to sleep like this," I said as I rolled over onto my stomach.

"Really not my problem," he said, then wrapped a cord around my wrist a couple of times, pulled it tight, and then wrapped my wrists together. "Perfect, now just a gentle reminder, you try anything stupid, and one of the brats gets it, understood?”

“Yeah sure, I hear you. Just let me say, again, this would be the perfect time for you to make tracks to some sunny beach or a distant mountaintop before the cops or those casino guys find you.”

“And let me say again, shut the hell up.”

# Thirty-five

I must have drifted off to sleep because it was dark when I awoke. I'd been lying on my side and had lost most of the feeling in my arms with the cord wrapped around my wrists. Right now, about the only thing I could feel was pain, very intense pain. My shoulders felt like they were about ready to pop out of the sockets.

A light was on in what I figured was the kitchen, not bright. I thought it might be the light over the stove or maybe some lights beneath the cabinets. We were lying on the floor, the three of us, Emma and Ava, on either side of me. A long, leather couch was down at my feet, blocking any view. Both the girls seemed to be asleep.

I could hear Carlos moving around in the dim light. It sounded like he opened the refrigerator and took something out. A moment later, I heard the familiar sound of a bottle cap getting popped off, and shortly after that, the sound of a bottle set down on the counter.

He was either singing to himself or he was having a conversation. I could hear his voice, but couldn't make out what he was saying and didn't pick up on another voice. It dawned on me he might be on the phone. I prayed he was making flight reservations and planned to just leave us here. I strained against the extension cord wrapped around my wrists but only succeeded in shooting waves of sharp pain up and down my arms.

I rolled over to face Emma and whispered in her ear. "Emma, Emma, wake up. Emma. Emma."

She wrinkled her nose and turned her head a little, then took a deep breath and returned to deep, rhythmic breathing.

"Emma, Emma honey, wake up. It's Dev, wake up, Emma."

Her eyes fluttered for a bit, and she said, "Dev?"

"Shhh-hhh, stay quiet. Can you try and untie my wrists?"

"Dev?"

"Shhh-hhh, quiet, honey."

She nodded.

"See if you can untie me," I whispered. I could hear Carlos again, still sounding like he was in a conversation. I rolled over with my back to Emma and moved my wrists to attract her attention. A moment later, I could feel her hands beginning to tug at the cord.

After some time, she said, "I can't do it, it's tied real tight. I can't get it off," she said.

"Keep trying, you're doing fine," I said, but the truth was she didn't know what she was doing and most likely couldn't see in the dark even if she did know what to do.

She tugged and pulled on the cord for a good few minutes, but nothing changed.

"I can't get it, Dev. I can't get it loose," she whispered.

"It's okay, good try. You go back to sleep, and we'll think of something else."

"I'm sorry, I just can't get it."

"That's okay, Emma. Go back to sleep, honey, it's okay."

She snuggled up against me and silently sobbed herself back to sleep. I went back to struggling against the cord and had even less luck.

I heard the refrigerator open three or four more times, always followed by the sound of a bottle being opened. I could only hope Carlos drank enough beer to pass out. At one point I heard him walk down a hallway and use the bathroom. On his way back he wandered in our direction and stared at us for a very long moment before he returned to the kitchen.

I drifted off to sleep again and woke to someone tugging at the cord around my wrists. I glanced over my shoulder and could just make out a determined look on Emma's little face. The dim light was still on in the kitchen area, but I couldn't hear anything that suggested life out there. With any luck Carlos, had drunk himself into a stupor, staggered out onto the balcony, and then gone over the railing.

Emma tugged and pulled, but didn't seem to be making any progress. I wiggled my hand and fingers in an effort to get the blood flowing, and suddenly, I felt a slight loosening of the cord. One length seemed to drop along the back of my hand. Emma stopped her effort for a moment then pulled the loosened section almost over my hand. I cupped my fingers, and she tugged the cord over my knuckles. That seemed to loosen another length, and she tugged that over my opposite hand. Suddenly I could feel the cord loosen, and Emma began to unravel everything from around my wrists.

It took her a few more minutes, but she was eventually able to pull the cord loose, and I slipped my wrist out. I lay on my back, unwrapped the remainder of the cord, then crossed my arms over my chest and began to massage them in an effort to get the blood flow back. I placed a finger to my lips signaling Emma to stay quiet.

She was still sitting up and nodded eagerly. I gently forced her down, then whispered in her ear, "Good job, Emma, very good. Now, close your eyes and pretend to be asleep just incase he checks on us."

She nodded eagerly then closed her eyes and smiled.

I continued to massage my arms and wiggle my fingers, all the while keeping an ear cocked for any hint of Carlos. Could we be so lucky that he took my thoughts to heart and just left? I didn't want to bet on it. I lay there for what seemed like an eternity, getting my arms back to a semblance of normal, and listening. I never heard a thing coming from beyond the leather couch.

I waited for what seemed like the better part of the night, wondering what in the hell I was going to do, then I slowly sat up and looked around in the dark. I closed one eye and looked into the dimly lit kitchen— no sign of Carlos, anywhere. I reached down and quickly began to undo the knotted cord around my ankles.

Once the cord was off, I massaged my ankles to get the blood flowing back into my feet. It took a while, but a sense of feeling gradually began to return. There was still no sign of Carlos.

I gradually got the layout of the place, at least the area we were in. I planned to scope out the living room where we were sleeping, then make my way to the kitchen. If he wasn't in the kitchen, I could grab the girls, and we could quietly get the hell out of here.

I grabbed the extension cord that had been wrapped around my legs and wound a length around either hand. If I found him asleep in the kitchen, I'd strangle the bastard, and then leave with the girls. I slowly crawled on my hands and knees around the edge of the leather couch. I closed one eye again and peered into the dimly lit kitchen. At least from the angle I was at, the kitchen appeared to be empty.

I scanned the darkened living room and dining area for any sign of him and came up empty-handed. I slowly got to my feet, took a couple of tentative steps, then made my way as quietly as possible toward the kitchen. I leaned against the open doorway and slowly peered around the corner. Unless Carlos was sleeping on the floor on the far side of the kitchen counter, the room was empty.

# Thirty-six

I checked the far side of the counter, just to be safe. Fortunately, he wasn't there. The counter was littered with seven beer bottles and what looked like a twist-off cap to a bottle, definitely not beer. I could only hope it was vodka and that he'd downed plenty of it.

I picked the cap up to smell it and suddenly heard a noise from the dark end of the condo. A distant door opened then a moment later a not so distant door closed. I remained where I was, afraid the sound of my heart thumping was going to give everything away. I heard the toilet flush, a door open, and then the very dimmest of lights attempted to drift across the oriental carpet only to be swallowed up by the murky darkness where we were sleeping, then all was quiet again.

I waited with the cord stretched between my hands, ready to charge into Carlos the moment he came through the kitchen door. I heard something that sounded like a footstep dragging, and suddenly, there was Carlos. A dark silhouette in the half light barely fifteen feet from me. He was just standing and looking over the leather couch down to the floor where the girls were sleeping in front of the fireplace,— the same place I was supposed to be. Only I was out here in the kitchen with my feet seemingly glued to the floor.

He seemed to stagger a half step as he stared toward the girls, then rubbed his eyes with the back of his hand. He held the Sig Sauer in the same hand, and suddenly, I was moving, cutting the distance between us in half.

A sober guy could have spun around and drilled me a half dozen times. Fortunately, I was dealing with Carlos. He appeared to be groggy and still feeling no pain. He staggered another step, and mumbled, "Wait, what the hell?" just before I slammed into him, and the Sig Sauer erupted.

My arms were crossed as we connected, and in one fell motion, I looped the cord around his neck, then pulled that sucker tight and held on as we tumbled over an end table, sending a table lamp crashing onto the floor in the process. The Sig Sauer fired as the lamp crashed, and the noise started the girls screaming. They sat wide-eyed with their arms wrapped around one another, frozen in the partial darkness as our two shadows thrashed and kicked around on the floor.

We rolled over on the floor two or three times until we were wedged up against the wall. Carlos was on top of me, and he slammed the back of his head into my mouth a couple of times. I rolled him off onto his side and jammed my knee up into the middle of his back then pulled on the cord even harder. I saw his arm crank the Sig Sauer over his head, and I shifted my head to the side just a moment before he fired. The muzzle flashed, and

I rolled us back and forth a couple of times in an attempt to slam his head into the wall.

The girls screamed. I pulled with all my might as he clawed at the cord around his neck trying to loosen it. I rolled him over on top of me and slammed his head into the baseboard trim. He continued to claw and groan at the cord wrapped firmly around his neck. I could hear him gurgle and croak, and he suddenly began to kick wildly. He waved the Sig Sauer and fired another round, this time into the ceiling.

The front door suddenly burst open, and a number of very large figures stormed into the room. Light flooded in from the illuminated hallway, but I was too focused on strangling Carlos to pay much attention.

Suddenly heavy paws ripped the cord out of my hands, and Carlos rolled off me, face down onto the floor gagging and gasping for air.

"I don't believe it, Haskell? You?"

Ava screamed from behind us, and 'Fat Freddy' jumped.

"Jesus Christ, are these the kidnapped kids?"

My ears were ringing, I had trouble hearing, and then a pair of hands lifted me up to my feet. I recognized the war shield tattoo with the eagle feathers, biceps the size of basketballs, and the pulled-back hair. He still wore the black T-Shirt that said 'SECURITY,' and he eyed me for a moment before he laughed and said, "No offense, dude, but you look like shit."

"Get him a towel or something. Christ, Haskell, you're dripping blood all over everything," Freddy said.

Carlos was still lying face down on the floor, inhaling deeply. The Sig Sauer rested a very long reach away against the wall. He looked like he was about to make a try for the thing when Freddy placed a black cowboy boot on his hand and then applied all three-hundred-and-fifty-plus pounds of weight.

"You are one stupid son-of-a-bitch, you know that?" Freddy said, looking down at Carlos.

Carlos groaned from all the weight on his hand.

Some guy came out of the bathroom with a wet washcloth and handed it to me. I dabbed it gently on my face and immediately pulled it away from my split lips. The cloth was covered with my blood.

"Relax, it probably looks worse than it really is, maybe go into the can and get cleaned up," Freddy said, then shifted his weight back onto Carlos's hand and ground his heel back and forth. It sounded like twigs snapping, and Carlos let out a deep, painful groan and grabbed his wrist with his free hand in an effort to pull it out from underneath Freddy's boot.

I took a step toward the bathroom, and the girls suddenly began to cry.

"Come on. You can come with me. These are our friends, they're gonna bring us back to your mom."

"We're gonna have to see Tubby first," Freddy said, "And we better get the hell out of here. You got about sixty seconds, then we gotta be making tracks."

The girls ran over to me, and we hurried into the bathroom. A glass rested on the sink, and I quickly filled it with water and then gingerly rinsed my mouth. I stupidly glanced in the mirror and barely recognized the bloodied creature staring back at me.

The swelling from two days ago had disappeared, and the bruises had turned a deep purple then morphed into a sickly brownish-green along the outer edges. My lips were swollen and looked like the victims of a very bad Botox injection, but the bleeding seemed to be subsiding. The girls turned around and stared at the tub and shower rather than watch me rinse my mouth out again.

"Let's go, Haskell," Freddy called from the living room.

I took the girls by the hand, and we hurried back down the front hall and out the door. I couldn't see Carlos anywhere.

As we hurried down the hallway toward the elevators, one of the doors to an adjacent unit began to open, and Freddy used a deep voice and said, "Police. Please lock your door and remain in your unit until we give you the all-clear."

I heard the click of a lock from inside the unit as we walked past. We quickly made our way down the hallway past the bank of elevators to the fire exit. "No cameras," Freddy said. "You able to do five flights?"

"I'd jump over the railing if it got us away from Carlos. Hey, just a minute, we forgot something," I said and ran back into the condo.

"Catch up, we're heading down," Freddy called after me.

I did a quick check of the living room, the kitchen, and the bathroom. I hurriedly looked through the master bedroom when suddenly, there was the pink suitcase just barely peeking out from under one of the pillows. I quickly opened it up, took two bundles of cash and stuffed them in my pockets then ran back out the door to catch up to Freddy. They were already two flights down. Fortunately the girls weren't able to go all that fast and I caught up to them just as they made it to the bottom, and we entered the main floor lobby together.

"I want my mommy," Ava cried as both she and Emma grabbed onto my hands.

"We're on our way, honey, don't worry. That bad man won't be bothering you anymore."

One of Freddy's thugs was already behind the wheel of the black Escalade with the motor running as we exited the building. Freddy quickly waddled ahead and opened the passenger door for us then oozed into the front seat. I lifted Ava into the backseat, Emma hopped in after her, and then I followed. I hadn't quite closed the rear door before we took off.

When we got to the security gate, the driver punched in a code from a piece of paper he held then floored it as soon as the gate opened. We hadn't been on Shepard Road for more than thirty seconds when a squad car with flashing lights appeared in the distance and shot past us, heading in the opposite direction toward The Peabody.

"We're gonna have to watch it, they're getting faster on their response times," the thug behind the wheel said to Freddy.

# Thirty-seven

We pulled into a small parking lot tucked behind The Derby. It was posted with a sign that simply read "PRIVATE" and was barely illuminated by a single light hanging over the metal door marked "Employees Only." In one of the busiest sections of town, the lot had six parking places, four of which were unoccupied, suggesting no one was stupid enough to challenge Tubby's privacy statement.

We pulled in front of three large dumpsters, as we piled out of the Escalade Ava asked, "Is mommy here?"

"We have to stop here for just a minute, and then they'll take us to mommy," I said. "That alright by you, Freddy?"

"Come on, we'll see what the boss wants," he said as the thug who had been driving punched a code into the back door of the building. There was an audible buzz and a snap, and then he held the door open for us. Freddy led the way up a set of steep, wooden stairs. The walls on either side of the stairs were painted a glossy dark grey up to maybe four feet, then a lighter grey from that point to the ceiling.

Emma followed behind Freddy, running her hand along the wall since there wasn't a handrail while I carried Ava and the pink suitcase.

The air held just the slightest hint of steak still lingering from the evening dinner trade along with maybe some roasted garlic and the strong scent of baking bread. I wasn't sure what time it was, but the streets had been pretty quiet on the ride over, so it had to be late.

Freddy was half-way down the hall by the time the girls and I made it to the top of the stairs. Light drifted out of an open door at the far end of the hallway, and we hurried in an attempt to catch up to Freddy. He knocked on the doorframe then waited for us to join him before he stepped inside. We followed a step or two behind him. Emma held tightly onto my hand with the suitcase.

The room was fairly large with a gas fireplace centered on one wall. Fancy dark oak paneling running maybe six feet up was wrapped around all four walls. The floor was covered in a dark burgundy carpet that was so thick I seemed to sink a little with every step. Two windows on the wall opposite the fireplace were covered with heavy, red velvet drapes. The drapes were edged with a dingy gold fringe that seemed to give the entire room a morbid look, not unlike a 1950's mortuary.

Centered between the two windows was an enormous, polished wood desk with vicious gargoyle heads carved into the corners. Behind the desk, holding a snifter of brandy and nibbling from a large plate of choco-late-covered pastry sat massive, red-faced, multi-chinned, Tubby Gustafson.

"Well, come in, come in, come in," Tubby called, spitting crumbs across the desk as he waved us forward. He stuffed the remainder of a pastry into his mouth then began to lick his fingertips as we approached.

Emma hung back, clinging even tighter to my hand. Ava tried to bury her head deeper into my shoulder.

"It's alright, don't be afraid, here, I've even got a special treat for you," Tubby said and pushed the pastry plate across the desk toward us.

He looked up at me and said, "I have to say, Haskell, the past couple of days have apparently done absolutely nothing to improve your appearance, good Lord. And you two little ladies must be the Emma and Ava that we've all been hearing so much about on TV. Now, which one of you is Emma?"

Emma grasped my hand a little tighter, stared at the floor, and said, "That's me."

"You're the oldest, aren't you? Here, sweetheart, how about a little nibbly?" Tubby said and leaned across the desk to hand her a pastry.

Emma cautiously took it from Tubby then examined it carefully.

"Go ahead, darling, taste it. They're very good."

She took a tiny bite then seemed to brighten after the first taste and took another larger bite.

"There, see, I knew you'd like it, they're one of my favorites. We make them here, right downstairs. It's," Tubby glanced cautiously around the room as if he were looking for spies hiding under the chairs before he spoke. He lowered his voice to almost a whisper and said, "It's a secret recipe, very secret."

Ava watched her sister take that large second bite, and although she still held on to me tightly, she cautiously glanced over at Tubby.

"And you must be, Ava, I bet you'd like one of these too, wouldn't you?" Tubby said, then raised the plate. Ava reached over and snatched a pastry then squirmed to indicate she wanted to be set down.

Tubby watched the girls with a look of satisfaction. It was as if he'd already gotten his good deed for the day out of the way in the wee hours of the morning, and he had the remainder of the day to misbehave. "Haskell?"

"None for me, I—"

"Don't kid yourself. I wasn't offering. They're for the children and me, besides, look at those lips, God, you're in no condition. Do you actually walk around like that, blood all over your shirt, you need a shave, no doubt a shower, and this is the kind of example you set for impressionable children?" Tubby said and shook his head.

"How did you find us?" I looked from Freddy to Tubby.

"Our friends up at the Grey Wolf, you might say we have a bit of working relationship." Tubby replied and then reached for another pastry. "Apparently, a car was stolen, a Mercedes, I believe, up on the north shore."

"Yeah, Carlos grabbed it from a couple, tied them up in their home, a pretty fancy place up on the North Shore, they—"

"That dude with the ponytail, he's part of the security team at the casino," Freddy said while Tubby crammed an entire pastry into his mouth, causing his cheeks to bulge like a chipmunk gathering nuts.

"Yeah, I thought I recognized him."

"You went all that way just to gamble? That seems crazy when you can lose your money just as easily right here in town," Tubby said, spraying more bits of pastry and chocolate across his desk.

"Not really, I followed Carlos up there, then, well, it's a long story, but I ended up with the girls, and Carlos stole that Mercedes."

"Like I was about to say, that guy from the casino, they were his folks, it was their Mercedes," Freddy chimed in as he settled into a chair over by the fireplace.

"Then they must have followed this," I said and took the transponder out of my pocket and placed it on Tubby's desk.

"Thing looks like a doorbell, what the hell is that?" Tubby asked.

"A transponder, it sends out a GPS signal, it's how they tracked the car, the Mercedes. Tracked us all the way down here in the cities, and it sent the signal they picked up when we were at The Peabody. I grabbed it out of the trunk of the Mercedes. See, we were locked in a basement and this naked, drunk woman on a coffee table—"

"Spare me the details," Tubby said, then reached for the largest pastry on the platter and crammed two-thirds of it into his mouth.

"So, Carlos O'Kelly?" I asked.

"I wouldn't worry about him," Freddy said.

"Speaking of which," Tubby said, licking his fingers and pointing to the pink suitcase.

I placed the suitcase on his desk, unzipped it, and then spun it around so it faced Tubby.

He slowly opened it up and stared for a long moment. Finally, he looked up, smiled at me for a half-second, and said, "Lovely." Then he zipped the suitcase closed, set it on the floor next to his chair, and grabbed another pastry.

"I think our deal was forty-eight hours, Haskell. You're late. However, under the circumstances, I'll let it go, this time. Girls, would you like another?" Tubby said and held out the plate of pastries to the girls.

They each snatched another one, then Emma said, "Can we go home, please?"

"I want to see my mommy," Ava said.

Tubby nodded and said, "A splendid idea, we'll take my car. Freddy, get a couple dozen of these pastries in a box for the girls, a treat to take along when we bring them home. Let me make a few quick phone calls first. Haskell, the bathroom's through that door over there.

You don't have a lot to work with, but try and maybe make yourself look half-way presentable."

# Thirty-eight

It was dark, and I guessed a good while past closing time based on how empty the streets were as we made our way toward Isabella's town-home. Both girls were sitting on my lap and snuggled tightly against me.

Tubby turned halfway round in the passenger seat and looked at me. The nice guy tone he'd used when sharing the chocolate pastry with the girls was gone, and he was back to his usual cranky self. "It's good the girls are safe, at least for now. The cops are gonna have a lot of questions. I think it would be wise if you didn't mention our involvement other than saving your sorry ass at The Peabody, got it?"

"But—"

"Don't say anything about O'Kelly dropping in at my card game, don't mention the car we loaned you?"

"Yeah, and don't mention my phone call to you about him picking up that chick at The Lumberyard. We don't need that kind of trouble. It will just bring more stupid questions," Freddy chimed in.

"We wouldn't want anything happening to these kids or their mother now, would we? Do we understand one another?" Tubby asked, not really waiting for an answer. "Good," he said a second later. He nodded, then turned around and stared out the window as we drove on in silence.

A few blocks from home Emma recognized the grocery store as we drove past, and she shouted, "Look, Ava, Kowalski's."

Ava blinked awake and seemed to come alive as she sat up straight and suddenly began to take in the familiar surroundings.

Two blocks later, Fat Freddy made a righthand turn onto Isabella's dark street. "You just shut the hell up and let me handle things, Haskell," Tubby said. "One can never have enough good PR. Besides, the way you look right now, you'll be lucky if they don't lock you up and just throw away the key." Both he and Freddy chuckled about that for the next couple of blocks until we approached a crowd of people gathered out in the street in front of Isabella's town-home.

"What's all this?" I said more to myself than anyone else. A half dozen news vans were parked along both sides of the street. All the lights were on in Isabella's. The news crews suddenly rushed towards us and swarmed around our moving vehicle.

"What in the hell would be the point of doing a good deed if no one knew about the damned thing?" Tubby said.

Freddy edged the Escalade through the crowd of news reporters and camera crews as he pulled over to the curb in front of Isabella's. The maple tree in front of her town-home had the faded yellow ribbon tied around the trunk. It was the same ribbon I'd had to take down a few years ago when Danny didn't make it back.

The crowd of reporters circled around the Escalade as Tubby pushed his door open and shouted, "We got, 'em. We got 'em. They're safe and sound ladies and gentlemen, safe and sound. I just couldn't sit back and watch. I felt we had to do something. My heart was breaking—"

"Mommy, mommy," both girls screamed in unison just as the front door flew open, and Isabella sailed down the front steps.

Emma kicked the car door open, and in an instant, Ava was off my lap jumping out the door behind her.

They wound up in a tight embrace in the small front yard, the three of them; Isabella, Emma, and Ava, no one letting go of the other. Two uniformed officers were trying to keep a semblance of order and failing miserably as the crowd of reporters and camera crews circled round and round. Tubby kept right on talking. Pandemonium reigned.

I saw my chance and quietly slipped out the far side of the car and into the street, side-stepping everyone as I made my way up Isabella's front steps and through her front door.

In short order, the cameras had turned from Isabella and the girls hugging, going back to Tubby, who was more than willing to hold court for as long as anyone cared to listen.

I didn't know how long I'd been asleep on the couch, fifteen minutes? An hour? I jerked awake when the door opened, and Isabella and the girls came in. They were still hanging on to one another, their faces stained with tears— only this time tears of joy.

"There he is," Isabella shouted as I sat up, and they all ran over and proceeded to hug me.

"Whoa, take it easy, ladies, one at time, one at a time," I said.

"Dev, thank you so much, thank you. I don't know how I'll ever be able to repay you. I can't, I, oh, thank you so much."

"It's been an interesting couple of days. I have to tell you the only reason we're here is because you've got two very brave girls here who never gave up and who helped me when we finally had a chance to get away."

The front door opened again, and Aaron LaZelle walked in, detective Jack Ditter followed behind him. Both were in jeans and sweaters and looked like they had driven over about three minutes after receiving the phone calls that no doubt woke them out of a sound sleep.

Isabella was on her feet and gave both cops a hug then rushed back over to the girls.

"We've got two uniforms at the door," Ditter said. "Right now, the best thing is to just get settled in with the girls, stay private. You can deal with the press tomorrow if you want. Believe me, they'll be anxious to talk to you."

"I don't know about that. I mean talking to them tomorrow. I just want the girls and—" Isabella started to cry and pulled the girls close to her, Ava wrapped her arms around her mother's thigh, and Emma hung onto her arm with both hands. "I'm sorry," Isabella said, but she couldn't seem to get any other words out.

"We'd like to talk to you. If you feel up to it," Aaron said to me.

I nodded then said to Isabella, "Do you still have those cold gel packs?"

"Oh, sorry, I'll get you one."

"No, that's okay. Are they in the freezer?"

"Yeah," she said then went back to hugging the girls.

"Let me just grab one, and we can get started," I said to Aaron.

"Probably be best if we did this downtown," Aaron said. "Officer Patty Ryan is on the way. She should be here in the next half hour. She'll stay with you tonight, make sure everyone is okay," he said to Isabella.

"It's late. I think I just want to give the girls a bath, and we'll all go to bed," she said.

"We'll keep the two guys out front, sometimes well, you probably know what the news media can be like by now."

Isabella nodded, and then looked at me. "You gonna be okay?"

"Not a worry."

"We just need to get Dev's version of the story. Apparently, Carlos O'Kelly is still out there somewhere," Ditter said then looked over at me for follow-up.

"He just ran off, I don't know where he went," I said.

"Oh, I can't thank you enough," Isabella said and gave me another long hug.

"Carlos won't be back to bother you," I whispered in her ear.

She gave me a kiss then, squeezed tightly and held on for a long moment before she pushed away.

"Thank you so much," she said.

"I'm just glad they're back safe and sound." I looked over at Ditter and Aaron, "Let's get started."

# Thirty-nine

At least it wasn't one of those cinderblock interview rooms. This was more of a conference room up in the homicide offices. I was on my third cup of lousy coffee, my second stale doughnut, and trying like hell to stay awake.

"So, you decided you would just head up to the Grey Wolf Casino to get away from everything going on down here?" Ditter asked for the umpteenth time.

"Yeah, that's about it."

"In all the years I've known you, I never knew you liked to gamble, Dev," Aaron said.

"I don't. I just thought I'd give it a try. You know?"

"And you met Carlos O'Kelly there?"

"Like I said before, not exactly, I saw his car, actually my car. He stole the thing from me if you remember. Anyway, he was driving by as I pulled into the parking lot, and so I just followed him."

"To a boat in Two Harbors?"

"Hey, look, guys, with all due respect. I'm going on about six hours of sleep for the past two or three days.

I'm pretty tired. The sun's coming up. You got everything on tape. I'd really like to go home and crash if that's okay."

"I guess that's fair," Aaron said. "I'll give you a lift. You can get some rest and then we'll have some more questions. I just haven't made up my mind yet."

"Made up your mind?"

"I can't determine if you're the luckiest or the unluckiest person in the world. And then there are our Federal friends. They'll have some questions for you as well."

"Oh, good."

"Come on, let's go, I'll drive you home. I think we could probably all use a break," Aaron said.

We were in his car, a Toyota SUV thing. Aaron had always been into classical music, and just now, he had some playing softly on the radio. It was all very relaxing, which had me on guard as he drove through downtown making his way to my place.

"So, you up for grabbing some breakfast before I drop you off?"

"You know, thanks, but I'd like to maybe take a raincheck. I'm really beat, Aaron, and I've been worrying about those two little girls since this whole thing first started. I need to start to decompress, and finally being able to grab some sleep will really help." Besides, I figured a breakfast with a side order of third-degree questions from Aaron didn't sound all that appealing.

"Yeah, sleeps probably a good idea, a long, hot shower wouldn't do you any harm, either."

"True."

"So tell me what really went down. How'd you know he was up at the Grey Wolf Casino?"

"Like I said before, I just went up there to get away from everything, and I saw him driving past in my car. Small world, isn't it?"

Aaron looked over at me and stared for a moment, but didn't bother to comment. We drove the next few minutes in silence until we pulled up in front of my place.

"Okay, home sweet home, dumb ass, here you go."

"Thanks, Aaron, I appreciate it, and I know you guys have worked hard on this thing, I'm just glad it's all over."

Aaron stared at me again for an uncomfortable length of time, like he was thinking of what to say. "I'm glad those little girls are safe, that was our first priority. I'm glad you're safe, Dev. You're a screw-up, but you're *our* screw-up. As for Carlos O'Kelly, given just the players we suspect, I have a strong suspicion we'll probably never hear from him again. I don't like that. It's not the way I operate. It certainly is not the way our legal system is designed to operate. That said, there's really not much I can do about that, at least not at this point."

I thought about giving him some rationalization. Rattle off my half baked story yet another time. I quickly settled for holding my hand out, and we shook. "Thanks for taking care of me, Aaron."

He just nodded, I climbed out, and he drove off. I still had to talk to the Feds, Detective Ditter would want to cover things again, but the girls were safe, I was safe and by extension, so was Tubby Gustafson, Fat Freddy, and that security guy from the Grey Wolf Casino.

# Forty

It was a big deal in town. The weather was unseasonably warm, and a number of reporters were there along with a number of cops, including Patty Ryan and Tai Vang. Aaron was there, of course, along with detective Ditter and a couple of other guys I recognized, but whose names I couldn't remember. We were all crowded into Isabella's town-home sipping bottles of water or cups of coffee. The Derby had sent over trays of cookies and pastries, but thankfully Tubby Gustafson and Fat Freddy were missing in action.

The girls had been home for a week, and I don't think they'd been more than a couple of feet from their mother in all that time. They seemed to be getting back to normal, and just now, they were arguing over a specific chocolate chip cookie, although a tray with another five or six dozen chocolate chip cookies sat on the table in front of them.

I had just shoved a miniature caramel roll into my mouth. The things were really good.

"How many of those things have you had? Someone else might like to eat one," Heidi said.

"Are you kidding? Come on, Tubby sent them over, and I'm just making sure they're safe for everyone else to eat."

"*You're* going to be called Tubby if you keep that up."

"Oh, I don't know, you haven't been complaining the last couple of nights."

"I'm just glad you're home and safe," she said, then squeezed my hand.

"Okay, everybody, we're about to get started, here, if I could have your attention," Isabella called out to the room. Gradually things quieted down until the only voice you heard was Ava.

"That's mine, that's the one I wanted, Emma."

That brought some laughter to the room, and then Isabella said, "As you all know, we've recently been through a very trying time. I really can't name all the people we owe so much to all of you who were there when the bottom fell out. All of you who worked so very hard, who never gave up. The wonderful people on the police force, Officers Patty Ryan and Tai Vang, Detective Jack Ditter, Mr. Gustafson, and just so very many people who never gave up. I can't tell you how, in the darkest of time, how very, very much—" and then she couldn't seem go on because she was so choked up.

"Oh, God, I'm so sorry. I promised myself I wouldn't do this and now look at me. It's just that without all of you, who helped in so many countless ways, well, we wouldn't be here today. There is one person in particular that I— that *we* owe a very special thanks to. He stepped up to the plate, and he's the reason we are back here as a family today."

People started to turn and stare at me. Heidi squeezed my hand. I reached for another caramel roll.

"I've known Dev Haskell since I was in ninth grade, a freshman in high school. In fact, I met my husband through him. He and Danny were friends, good friends. In 2011, I asked Dev to take down the yellow ribbon on the tree out front when we got word Danny wasn't coming home. He's been here ever since, in the background, but always there if I ever needed anything. And I have no doubt that things would have been a lot worse that night if I'd been home to answer the door instead of Dev."

"He promised me he would get the girls back. And he did. He was beaten, injured, shot at, and I, I can't really thank him enough and so I'll just ask one more favor. Dev, would you please go outside and take down that ribbon. This time they came home, this time they made it back, and we're, we're all—" And then she just started sobbing.

"Dev," Heidi whispered and squeezed my hand.

I quickly made my way through the crowd and wrapped my arms around Isabella. I felt her shudder slightly, and I kissed her on the forehead.

She pulled away after a moment and said, "Oh God, I'm so not good at this," then she blew her nose into a Kleenex.

"How romantic," I said, everyone chuckled, and more than a few Kleenex's came out.

"I'm gonna need some help here. Emma, Ava, come on and give me a hand," I said.

The girls took my hands, and we walked out the door, a couple of camera crews were already outside in position. The place emptied as everyone followed out behind us, and we walked toward the maple tree as one large mob.

The faded yellow ribbon was still wrapped around the tree, and I said, "If Emma here hadn't helped, we wouldn't be here today. So, Emma, if you'd do the honors, here," I said then I lifted Emma up so she could untie the ribbon.

"What about me?" Ava asked, which brought laughter from the crowd.

Emma nodded to me, and I set her down and picked up Ava, "Ava gave us both the support we needed to keep on. Without the two of them, these two wonderful sisters, we wouldn't be here."

Ava pulled the ribbon off the tree, gave me a kiss, and handed the ribbon to her mother. Isabella clutched the ribbon tightly against her chest, and the girls wrapped themselves around their mother.

It was quiet for a long moment, and then Isabella said, "Come on back inside, we've got plenty to eat."

We chatted, sipped more coffee, shook all sorts of hands, and gradually the crowd began to thin out until it was just family and Heidi and me. "Girls, I love you, but it's time for me to go home."

"You could take a bath with us," Ava said.

Isabella's mother shot me a glance.

"Maybe some other time, right now I need to go home, I'm very tired." We lingered for another ten minutes, said our goodbyes, and then we were out the door.

"Wow," Heidi said as I pulled her car away from the curb.

"Yeah, that was nice."

"Nice? Dev, you're going to be on the news tonight and in tomorrow's paper, again. Nice? It was unbelievable."

"You want to grab some dinner."

"No."

"No?"

"First of all, you ate more of those caramel rolls than anyone else who was there. You can't possibly have room for dinner. And then, to be honest, I just want to go home and hold you. Sometimes you can fool everybody, even me, into thinking you're just a really nice guy."

# The End

Thank you for taking the time to read **Yellow Ribbon**. If you enjoyed the book, please tell your friends and family. Thanks again. My best to you and yours.
Mike


Don't miss the following sample of the next work of genius in the Dev Haskell series, **Dog Gone**.

# Sneak Peek

# Dog Gone

## Second Edition

## MIKE FARICY

# One

It was one of those intimate moments— sort of.

"Oh, Dev. Oh, Dev. Yes! Yes!" Maddie's voice ratcheted up with passionate excitement.

She was a beautiful, blue-eyed, natural blonde, with a gorgeous figure, sexy southern drawl, and a fascinating little lacy tattoo across the small of her back. At the moment, her back was arched, so just her heels and shoulders were touching the mattress on the four-poster bed. Her head was hanging partially over the side, and her eyes had that faraway look like she'd been transported to a very magical place. The three of us were sharing an intimate moment, Maddie, me, and apparently Morton.

Morton was her dog. A three year old Golden Retriever the color of a peanut butter cookie who, at the moment, was busily licking Maddie's face.

Even I found it impossible to maintain concentration and finally rolled over on my side next to Maddie. "I'm not sure I'm comfortable working with an audience," I said.

She laughed, and Morton poked me in the back of the head with his cold nose.

"He's a people dog."

"A people dog?"

"Yeah, he likes people, in fact, he probably thinks he's a person, and he wants to be involved."

"That might be okay if we were taking a walk, but this is—"

Her phone rang. It was just after midnight. Experience had taught me nothing good ever comes from a phone call at this hour.

Maddie rolled off the bed, gave Morton a pat on the head, picked her jeans up off the floor, and dug the cell out of her back pocket.

"Oh, wow, it's my dad," she said, sounding puzzled then answered. "Dad? Hey, is everything okay?"

I sat up and leaned against the carved wooden headboard.

"Oh? You're kidding, when? Where is she now?" Maddie said, looking worried as she sat down on the edge of the bed.

She listened for a few moments, occasionally interjecting a one-word response. "Yes. No. Yes. Possibly…." Eventually, she said, "No, Dad, I need to be there. I'll book a flight and be down in the morning. No, don't be silly, it's not a problem. I need to be there. Yes, Midtown? On Peachtree? No, I'll grab a cab. No, now not another word. I'll see you in the morning. Love you. Yes. Okay, bye, bye."

"Everything okay?" I said stupidly.

"Not really, that was my dad. Apparently, my mom was in a bike accident and broke her hip. She's okay, they've got her in Emory University Hospital, but I need to get down to Atlanta. Dad's worthless at this kind of thing."

I knew for a fact that Maddie's dad had started with nothing and now ran a number of very successful firms doing business in Georgia, Alabama, and Florida. I doubted he was worthless at this or anything else. I also knew enough not to offer that opinion. "Anything I can do to help?"

She walked over to her desk and turned on the computer, then pulled a sexy little black silk robe from the back of her bedroom door and slipped it on. The robe had red piping along the edge and around the button-holes, and barely fell to her thigh with slits along the side up to her hip bone. I liked it a lot.

"I'm going to have to book a flight for tomorrow. I'll have to take Morton."

"Morton? You're kidding." At the sound of his name, Morton's tail kicked into overdrive, and he looked back and forth from Maddie to me, panting with his tongue hanging out.

"Well, I can't very well leave him on his own. He doesn't like boarding in a kennel. Like I said, he thinks he's a person, not a dog."

"Maddie, nothing against Morton, but he's going to present one more complication you don't need right now. Not to mention your folks."

"They like him, maybe, I think."

"I'm sure they do, but when your mom gets out of that hospital, you're going to need to focus on her and your dad. Morton's going to be in a strange environment. It's just not the best idea. What if he jumps on her? Or what if he tries to lick her or something and she falls?"

"I had him at the Bed and Biscuit for a weekend, but that didn't work out too well."

"Bed and Biscuit?"

"It's a place to board your dog, but he somehow got into the same kennel as this high-bred female Collie and well...."

"What did he do, bite the thing?"

"Not exactly, I guess she was in heat, and he maybe might have impregnated her."

"But that can't be his fault, he can't help it, he's a guy."

She rolled her eyes, then said, "That argument doesn't really help. The kennel ended up having to pay damages and more or less nicely told me not to bring Morton back, ever again. I don't think he does very well in that kind of environment, anyway."

"I just think it's not the best idea, bringing him to your folks right now."

"Well, what else can I do?" She was online now, clicking keys, she pulled a billfold out of the purse at her feet and rifled through it to get a credit card.

"Don't you know someone? You must have a friend who could take him? You're only going on a short trip. What? A couple of days, tops?"

"Only a day or two, problem is just about everyone I can think of already has a dog or a couple of cats, and Morton doesn't really like other dogs, and he hates cats. His therapist said he just doesn't like to share the spotlight."

Therapist? "Well, there must be someone you can think of."

She was inputting her credit card number and understandably seemed focused on the computer screen at the moment. She clicked a few more keys, and suddenly, her printer fired up.

"There's my boarding pass. Nine o'clock flight tomorrow morning. Hey, I've got an idea," she said and stood up with a devilish grin on her face. As she turned to face me, she undid the little silk robe and pulled it back, placing her hands on her hips, completely exposing herself in the process. She was trimmed in the shape of a martini glass with a tattoo of what looked like Morton's head peeking out of the glass.

I felt my pulse ratchet up, but I think it was from the wave of panic spreading over me, "Oh no, no, that would be a bad idea. A really bad idea."

"What?" She said and slowly strutted around the end of the bed toward me with her hands still on her hips. She moved her shoulders from side to side with every step, and my eyes began tracking her breasts as they bounced and swayed back and forth.

"I, I can't take him. I wouldn't know what to do. I don't know the first thing about taking care of a dog."

"He really likes you. Y'all are kind of alike in some ways, you know, immature, irresponsible, somewhat lazy and in need of training and an awful lot of direction. Both of you tend to be bad boys," she said and then slipped the silk robe off her shoulders, letting it fall to her waist.

"Maddie, this isn't fair."

"What? Is it my fault I suddenly can't seem to help myself? Can't seem to get enough of you?" she said and licked her lips suggestively. "You just seem to have that effect on me, Dev. God only knows what I'm liable to do. You know how I get when I really, really want something. I'm liable to do anything, absolutely anything." Her eyes seemed to project heat, and she stuck her tongue out ever so slightly and moved it back and forth between her sensuous lips.

The silk robe suddenly dropped to the floor, and she ran a hand down my foot to the ankle then slowly started to walk her fingers up my leg. "Guess - what - I - really - really - want - right - now?"

"Don't do this…."

# TWO

She handed me a multi-paged document that was stapled in the upper left corner. The cover sheet just said 'MORTON,' and the second page was an index.

"So, I typed instructions up this morning while you were still asleep. This has everything you'll need."

It was a little before seven in the morning, and the day already seemed to be headed down the drain. I had just pulled into the entrance to Terminal One at the Minneapolis/St. Paul airport. The taxi behind me leaned on his horn as I merged into the lane marked departures.

"I typed out his schedule. It's on page two. It's pretty simple. He just needs a little walk, twice a day, maybe just an hour or so in the morning and then again in the evening. On page three, I've got his vet listed and then a backup just in case. His therapist is over on Marshall Ave., Morton has his regular therapy appointment on Thursday, at two, don't be late. I better make a note to email you a reminder," she said, typing with her thumbs as she input something on her cellphone.

"I've got his food schedule on page four. The green bag is for the evening, the tan one for the morning. One-

and-a-quarter cups for both servings, please no additives or scraps, he's got a number of allergies. I find he does a lot better if I sit on the floor and have breakfast and dinner with him."

"Which dog food is your favorite?"

She ignored me. "Oh, and *do not feed him from the table*. It's bad for him in so many ways. While you were asleep, I put his food and water dishes and his favorite chew toys on the floor of the back seat. I taped the prescription bottle with his heart worm pills to his morning food bag, that's when he gets the pill, every morning. You should grind up his heart worm pill and sprinkle it on his food. He won't eat the pill if you just put it in his dish. I try and feed him about ten minutes after seven in the morning. I find he does best if you keep him on that schedule. Don't forget. His blood pressure meds are taped to the evening food bag. Just half a pill, fifteen minutes before he eats, that's in my notes, too, so don't worry. I put his bed in the trunk of your car. He'll probably be most comfortable sleeping in your bedroom. It's good Feng Shui if he's aligned with the window and the sun. Oh, and his favorite TV show is "The Voice.""

"TV show?" I said as I pulled in front of the main terminal.

"Yeah, "The Voice," you know the reality show with Tom Jones? He really likes the singers. Hey, I'm flying Delta, and I already have my boarding pass. I've just got carry-on so you can drop me off anywhere, all I have to do is clear security."

I pulled to the curb in front of the next entrance. "You just take care of your mom, and don't worry about Morton. He'll be fine."

She turned around and knelt on the passenger seat then put on a sexy face.

My first thought was this probably isn't the best place for more kink, but....

"Oh, good-bye, Morton," she said in her high pitched, little-girl Morton voice. "Now you behave and take good care of Dev while I'm gone. I'll be back just as soon as I can. I'll call you every day, so we can talk." Then she wrinkled her nose and let Morton lick her all over her face. She leaned over and gave me a quick peck on the cheek, rubbing a heavy dose of Morton drool along the side of my face in the process.

"Oh, I just know you two are going to have fun. Okay, see you later boys," she said from out on the side-walk then she slammed the car door closed and headed into the terminal.

# Three

When I edged away from the curb, Morton immediately started whining. As I picked up speed, he began barking and pacing back and forth looking out the rear window. His wagging tail kept hitting me in the back of my head.

"Okay, settle down back there, Morton. Settle down." At the sound of his name, the tail began to wag even faster against the back of my head.

"Morton, damn it," I shouted and reached behind to shove him over. A horn blast from alongside got me to swerve back into my lane. The guy sped up, gave me the finger as he sailed past and took off down the road. The remainder of our drive home was uneventful.

I pulled into my driveway, then opened the passenger door and grabbed Morton by the collar. I walked him up to the front door, opened it and let him inside, then walked back to the car and began unloading everything Maddie had packed up. I put Morton's bed in the kitchen, set the food bags in the pantry, tossed his chew toys on the kitchen floor, and filled his water dish. I left the single-spaced multi-page instructions on the kitchen counter, closed the swinging door that led to the dining room, and drove down to my office.

Maddie phoned about an hour later. "How's it going?"

"I'm doing fine, still in the recovery mode from our love session last—"

"I meant, Morton."

"Oh, great, not a problem."

"Really?" She sounded more than a little surprised.

"Yeah, he's just taking it easy," I said. I didn't want to let her know he was locked in the kitchen back at my place.

"Can I talk to him?"

"What?"

"Let me talk to him. Just put the phone by his ear. We do it all the time."

"We?"

"Yeah, Morton and me. Come on, we're about to board, and I'm going to have to turn this off in a few moments."

"Okay, hang on," I said then sat at my desk for a long moment listening.

"Hi Morton, hi Morton, miss me?" Maddie said in that screwy, high pitched, little girl Morton voice.

I panted into the phone. Just as I barked, the office door opened, and my office mate, Louie, walked in.

"What the hell?"

I put a finger to my lips, signaling Louie to be quiet then panted some more.

"Okay, bye, Morton, bye, bye, bye," Maddie said.

"Wow, he really seems to know who's on the phone. He looks really happy," I said.

"I knew it. Thanks again, Dev. I really appreciate it."

"Not a problem," I lied. "Hey, best to your folks. I'll see you whenever you return."

"Thanks, I'm stepping onto the plane now, so I'm going to ring off. Bye, bye, bye," she said, sounding very happy.

"What the hell was that? You're seeing a woman with a dog fetish?"

"You wouldn't believe it."

"Try me," Louie said as he tossed his computer case onto his picnic table desk.

I told him the story about Maddie's late-night phone call, her booking the flight, and not having anyone to take care of Morton. I left out the part about her unique, payment in advance plan.

"I never figured you for being much of a pet kind of guy."

"I'm not, but it just seemed like she didn't have any other options. She was under pressure, and well, I just thought it would be the right thing to do and help her out."

"Never figured you for the caring, sensitive type, either."

# Four

I worked the rest of the day checking out references listed on a series of job applications for a position at an insurance company. It was boring drudgery, but it paid the bills, at least some of them. Occasionally, I scanned the apartment building across the street with my binoculars, hoping the two girls on the third floor might be home early. They weren't.

"You give any thought to heading over to The Spot for just one?" Louie asked it was getting close to five.

"I could use it, it's been a long day," I said, placing the binoculars back on the window sill and turning my computer off.

Louie looked up from his legal pad. "Oh, you're set to go right now? Let me just finish this section, and I'll catch up, shouldn't be more than five or ten minutes."

Mike was tending bar, and he'd just set my third beer down in front of me. I was drinking an Abel, a new micro-brewery in town when Louie finally showed up. "Sorry about that. Just got a call from a former client, his third DUI."

"Oh-oh, not good."

"Yeah, add to that the assault charge when he took a swing at the arresting officer, and he's going away for a while."

"Why did he call you if he's a former client?"

"He wasn't *former* when he called. I just fired him ten minutes ago. Guy's abusive, obnoxious, still under the influence plus he never paid me for the last time I represented him."

"Charming."

We chatted for a while. Louie bought a round then I bought a round. My phone rang, and I made the mistake of answering without checking the caller id. Some guy behind us was just in the process of loading up the juke-box.

"Hi, Dev, let me talk to Morton."

"Hey, Maddie, how are things going?"

"Where are you?"

"Me? Oh, I'm just out running a quick errand. I wanted to pick up some of these rawhide chews for Morton. I thought he might like them." Bob Seger fired up on the jukebox behind me. Mike was clearing away our empty glasses.

Louie looked at me and shook his head in disgust.

"Sounds like you're in a bar."

"No, just some kids driving by playing the radio too loud," I said, slipping off my stool and heading out the side door.

"You're not leaving him alone, are you? He needs his walk for starters, and then social interaction."

"We already went for his walk," I lied. "Really fun, and I'm just heading back home, should be there in about fifteen minutes."

"Okay, I'll call back then," she said and hung up.

I went back inside, threw some cash on the bar for a tip, then said, "I gotta run, man. I forgot all about this dog sitting gig. And she's going to be calling back in fifteen minutes."

Louie snorted and said, "Sounds like you're the one on the leash."

I was busy cleaning up the kitchen when Maddie called back. Morton had peed on the floor more than once. He'd gotten into the pantry, dragged both dog food bags out, and scattered the contents all over the kitchen floor. He'd chewed up one of the legs on a kitchen stool and pulled a loaf of bread off the kitchen counter and ate the entire thing.

Maddie called while I was down on my hands and knees, attempting to separate the two different types of dog food spread all over the kitchen floor. Morton's tail started wagging as soon as my phone rang.

"Put him on," she said.

I thought about putting him on a plane down to Atlanta but then held the phone up to Morton's ear. His tail wagged back and forth, and he barked a couple of times. I could hear her saying dopey things in that ridiculous voice she used with him. After a couple of minutes, I put the phone back up to my ear as she continued. "Did you have a fun day, Morton? Are you on a little vacation?"

"There you go," I said, trying not to sound too pissed off.

"Sorry if I was crabby before, I figured you were probably out in some sleazy bar. Does he like the rawhide chew?"

"I didn't want to give him one until after you called, you know, so he wouldn't be interrupted."

"Oh, that's so sweet."

"Yeah, that's me. How are your folks doing?"

"Pretty good, hopefully, Mom will be discharged in a day or two. I'll hang on for about twenty-four hours to get them sorted after that, and then I should be able to come back home."

I looked around at my destroyed kitchen. Great, just two or three more days of coming home to this. "Okay, no rush, just keep us posted."

"Thanks, Dev. I know he's in good hands."

Yeah, I thought, and those hands are about to be wrapped around his neck. "Talk to you later, Maddie."

"Okay, bye, bye, bye," she said and hung up, sounding a lot happier.

I looked around at the mess. If I was honest, it was at least partially my fault, I mean, Maddie had the poor guy seeing a therapist for God's sake, and I'd completely forgotten about him. He stood opposite me, staring and no doubt conjuring up his next stunt. I had a better idea.

"Come on, Morton, let's go for a walk."

## To be continued...

As unbelievable as it sounds, things are going to get even crazier! Talk about stepping in it, and with Morton! Better grab a copy of **Dog Gone**, and help out Dev and Morton… They're going to need it!

# Books by Mike Faricy
## Crime Fiction Firsts

**A boxset of the first four books in four crime fiction series:**

Russian Roulette; Dev Haskell series
Welcome; Jack Dillon Dublin Tales series
Corridor Man; Corridor Man series
Reduced Ransom! Hot Shot series

**The following titles comprise the Dev Haskell series:**
Russian Roulette: Case 1
Mr. Swirlee: Case 2
Bite Me: Case 3
Bombshell: Case 4
Tutti Frutti: Case 5
Last Shot: Case 6
Ting-A-Ling: Case 7
Crickett: Case 8
Bulldog: Case 9
Double Trouble: Case 10
Yellow Ribbon: Case 11
Dog Gone: Case 12
Scam Man: Case 13
Foiled: Case 14
What Happens in Vegas… Case 15
Art Hound: Case 16
The Office: Case 17

Star Struck: Case 18
International Incident: Case 19
Guest From Hell: Case 20
Art Attack: Case 21
Mystery Man: Case 22
Bow-Wow Rescue: Case 23
Cold Case: Case 24
Cash Up Front: Case 25
Dream House: Case 26
Alley Katz: Case 27
The Big Gamble: Case 28
Bad to the Bone: Case 29
Silencio!: Case 30
Surprise, Surprise: Case 31
Hit & Run: Case 32
Suspect Santa: Case 33
P.I. Apprentice: Case 34
Rebel Without a Clue: Case 35


**The following titles are Dev Haskell novellas:**
Dollhouse
The Dance
Pixie
*Fore!*
Twinkle Toes
(*a Dev Haskell short story*)

**The following are Dev Haskell Boxsets:**
Dev Haskell Boxset 1-3
Dev Haskell Boxset 4-6
Dev Haskell Boxset 7-9
Dev Haskell Boxset 10-12
Dev Haskell Boxset 13-15
Dev Haskell Boxset 16-18
Dev Haskell Boxset 19-21
Dev Haskell Boxset 22-24
Dev Haskell Boxset 25-27
Dev Haskell Boxset 28-30
Dev Haskell Boxset 1-7
Dev Haskell Boxset 8-14
Dev Haskell Boxset 15-19
Dev Haskell Boxset 20-24
Dev Haskell Boxset 25-29


**The following titles comprise the Jack Dillon Dublin Tales series:**
Welcome
Jack Dillon Dublin Tale 1
Sweet Dreams
Jack Dillon Dublin Tale 2
Mirror Mirror
Jack Dillon Dublin Tale 3
Silver Bullet
Jack Dillon Dublin Tale 4
Fair City Blues
Jack Dillon Dublin Tale 5

Spade Work
Jack Dillon Dublin Tale 6
Madeline Missing
Jack Dillon Dublin Tale 7
Mistaken Identity
Jack Dillon Dublin Tale 8
Picture Perfect
Jack Dillon Dublin Tale 9
Dublin Moon
Jack Dillon Dublin Tale 10
Mystery Woman
Jack Dillon Dublin Tale 11
Second Chance
Jack Dillon Dublin Tale 12
Payback Brother
Jack Dillon Dublin Tale 13
The Heist
Jack Dillon Dublin Tale 14
Jewels To Kill For
Jack Dillon Dublin Tale 15
Retirement Scheme
Jack Dillon Dublin Tale 16
The Collector
Jack Dillon Dublin Tale 17

**Jack Dillon Dublin Tales Boxsets:**
Jack Dillon Dublin Tales 1-3
Jack Dillon Dublin Tales 4-6
Jack Dillon Dublin Tales 1-5

Jack Dillon Dublin Tales 1-7
Jack Dillon Dublin Tales 6-10

**The following titles comprise the Hotshot series;**
Reduced Ransom! Second Edition
Finders Keepers! Second Edition
Bankers Hours Second Edition
Chow Down Second Edition
Moonlight Dance Academy Second Edition
Irish Dukes (Fight Card Series)
*written under the pseudonym Jack Tunney*

**The following titles comprise the Corridor Man series:**
Corridor Man
Corridor Man 2: Opportunity knocks
Corridor Man 3: The Dungeon
Corridor Man 4: Dead End
Corridor Man 5: Finger
Corridor Man 6: Exit Strategy
Corridor Man 7: Trunk Music
Corridor Man 8: Birthday Boy
Corridor Man 9: Boss Man
Corridor Man 10: Bye Bye Bobby

**Corridor Man novellas:**
Corridor Man: Valentine
Corridor Man: Auditor
Corridor Man: Howling

Corridor Man: Spa Day

**The following are Corridor Man Boxsets:**
Corridor Man Boxset 1-3
Corridor Man Boxset 1-5
Corridor Man Boxset 6-9

**All books are available on Amazon.com**
**Thank you!**

**Contact the author:**
- Email: mikefaricyauthor@gmail.com
- Twitter: @Mikefaricybooks
- Facebook: Mike Faricy Author
- Website: http://www.mikefaricybooks.com

**Published by**

**MJF Publishing**